ON I

STEPHEN GREGORY (b. 1952) was born in Derby, England, and earned a degree in law from the University of London. He worked as a teacher for ten years in various places, including Wales, Algeria, and Sudan, before moving to the mountains of Snowdonia in Wales to write his first novel, *The Cormorant* (1986), which won Britain's prestigious Somerset Maugham Award and drew comparisons to Poe. The book was also adapted for film as a BBC production starring Ralph Fiennes. Two more novels, both set in Wales, followed: *The Woodwitch* (1988) and *The Blood of Angels* (1994). His work attracted the notice of Oscar-winning director William Friedkin (*The Exorcist*), and he spent a year in Hollywood working on stories and scripts. More recently, he has published *The Waking That Kills* (2013), *Wakening the Crow* (2014), and *Plague of Gulls* (2015).

BY STEPHEN GREGORY

The Cormorant (1986)*

The Woodwitch (1988)*

The Blood of Angels (1994)*

The Perils and Dangers of this Night (2008)

The Waking That Kills (2013)

Wakening the Crow (2014)

Plague of Gulls (2015)

On Dark Wings: Stories (2019)*

* Published by Valancourt Books

ON DARK WINGS

stories by

STEPHEN GREGORY

VALANCOURT BOOKS

On Dark Wings by Stephen Gregory
First edition 2019

Copyright © 2019 by Stephen Gregory

Published by Valancourt Books, Richmond, Virginia
http://www.valancourtbooks.com

ISBN 978-1-948405-41-6 (*hardcover*)
ISBN 978-1-948405-42-3 (*trade paperback*)

Also available as an electronic book.

All Valancourt Books publications are printed on acid free paper
that meets all ANSI standards for archival quality paper.

Set in Dante MT

CONTENTS

To Catch a Thief   7

Celandine and Periwinkle   12

The Cormorant   35

Twice Bitten   43

Lingering   51

The Boys Who Wouldn't Wake Up   54

The Dreaming Pig   79

The Theatre Moth   86

The Drowning of Colin Henderson   95

The Late Mr Lewis   99

The Devil Bird   104

The Blackbird's Song   110

The Progress of John Arthur Crabbe   120

Dreamcatcher   126

'To Catch a Thief' originally appeared in *Illustrated London News*, Dec. 1, 1980.

'Celandine and Periwinkle' and 'Dreamcatcher' are new tales written specially for this volume.

'The Cormorant' originally appeared in *Illustrated London News*, Dec. 5, 1983.

'Twice Bitten', 'Lingering', 'The Dreaming Pig' and 'The Theatre Moth' are previously unpublished.

'The Boys Who Wouldn't Wake Up' originally appeared in *The Valancourt Book of Horror Stories, Vol. 2* (Valancourt Books, 2017).

'The Drowning of Colin Henderson' originally appeared in *The Beauty of Death 2: Death by Water* (Independent Legions Publishing, 2017).

'The Late Mr Lewis' originally appeared in *North Wales Magazine* in 2017.

'The Devil Bird' originally appeared in *Anglo-Welsh Review*, No. 79 in 1985.

'The Blackbird's Song' originally appeared in *Woman & Home* in 1987.

'The Progress of John Arthur Crabbe' originally appeared in *Illustrated London News*, Dec. 6, 1982.

TO CATCH A THIEF

As you go into the village on your way to Dartmoor there is a row of old almshouses. About 100 yards farther on, on the left-hand side of the street, there is the wildlife gallery and tea shop owned by my father. During the winter there is not much trade but from spring until late autumn we are always busy. Downstairs in the two front rooms we serve morning coffee and afternoon tea. The customers sit surrounded by hundreds of antiques, curios and trinkets, hunting horns, horse brasses, little bells and rings, odds and ends and bric-a-brac. Some of the items are real antiques but others are not worth much. When the customers have had their tea or coffee they usually browse round the paintings in our wildlife gallery.

There are two other rooms downstairs and three big rooms upstairs, all full of pictures by local artists and all of animals, birds, trees or flowers. Mostly they are the kind of wildlife we see on the moor and around the village: otters, badgers, foxes, hawks and owls. More often than not the customers from the tea room leave without buying a picture, but then they come back regularly and seem to enjoy browsing in the gallery. That is not to say we never sell a picture; in fact during the summer there is a fairly regular turnover.

We are always losing small items to light-fingered customers. It is easy for someone who is tempted by

7

a little brass or other trinket to pocket it when no one is looking. There are only a couple of waitresses in the downstairs front rooms and they are usually busy. Notices in the gallery and tea shop threaten prosecution for anyone found pilfering, but things are still stolen, especially during the hectic summer weeks. My father keeps a sharp look-out and occasionally confronts a suspected thief. Sometimes he is right and there is a scene of stammering confusion and even tears; the item is returned and the customer leaves in shame. But when father is wrong, then it is he who must apologize and resign himself to losing a customer.

Something strange happened a few years ago. We had the usual variable weather but we still did a reasonable amount of business. Among the paintings that covered the walls of the upstairs rooms my favourite was the heron, finely detailed, stalking across a pool ready to spear an unsuspecting trout. He was just like our own heron, a regular visitor to the garden pond. My father cursed him long and hard for making off with a fat goldfish. But I liked him and I liked the picture. Downstairs was a wonderful picture of a pair of magpies. Whereas all the other creatures in the room were minutely drawn, sharp in every feather or whisker, the magpies seemed a bit dusky and vague. They confronted each other among the soft branches of an oak which disappeared mistily behind them.

That season a lot of trinkets had vanished. After a busy week when customers had been bustling in and out for tea, fingering the brasses and horns and scrutinizing the paintings, we would often miss small attractive pieces. It made my father furious and each time he would vow to watch out and catch the thief at the next opportunity. But the days went by and apart from a couple of embarrassing confrontations with large, moist ladies or tearful girls we were not sharp enough to stop the steady flow of disappearing objects. The police were called in several times and hovered round in uniform or plain clothes, but this did nothing to improve the situation. Staff and customers became uneasy and business tailed off until we had to abandon the idea. The number of missing items increased, which vexed my father and left the baffled police inspector shuffling his heavy shoes into the carpet.

I was intrigued. Working around the gallery every day of my school holiday I felt I knew it better than anybody. I watched people closely, even the waitresses and my father. Sometimes I wondered whether I was under suspicion myself. But however intently I stared at customers and studied their movements I never caught a glimpse of anything that vaguely resembled criminal behaviour. More and more items of jewelry and brass curios vanished.

One night as I was lying awake in my bedroom on the second floor I decided to go down to the first floor and browse about. It was relaxing to pad about in my slippers and dressing-gown, beaming the torch up onto the pictures, or just to stand by the windows and enjoy the eerie atmosphere of moonlight, silence and the unblinking creatures around the walls. I went downstairs as quietly as I could, knowing which creaky steps to avoid and running my hand ahead of me down the bannister, until I came to the narrow landing. Then I turned into the large exhibition room on my left.

I sat down in a leather armchair and flashed the torch around the room. The otters and foxes seemed flat and lifeless under the beam, but the badgers wanted to romp across their canvasses. They thrust their stripey snouts at me and ambled about like dusty old clerks in a gloomy office. Farther round the room the heron was poised over the still waters of the pool. The torchlight picked out his yellow eye and a line of metallic blue along the murderous beak. On the opposite wall a barn owl ghosted over the canvas like a giant moth. Outside a tawny owl bubbled out a quavering hoot. Then I must have fallen asleep.

I woke up cold and stiff. The torch lay across my lap, still sending a pool of light on to the carpet. A noise was coming from the room below. Making sure I was properly awake, I stood up and wrapped the dressing-gown tightly round me. I went slowly downstairs, listening. Before I had covered the distance from the foot of the stairs to the door of the exhibition room I heard the noise again. I turned off the torch and stood still until my eyes became used to the gloom.

Sure enough, from within the room came the irregular sounds I had heard from my armchair. There would be a period of complete silence and then a sudden flurry of soft activity, a sort of gentle beating. After that, an occasional scratch on woodwork and the clink of metal objects. There may have been a chuckle though I do not expect you to believe me. I took several steps forward and turned to stand in the doorway.

One of the magpies was perched on the sideboard by the windows. The moonlight fixed it with its brightness, emphasizing the contrast of black and white. In its beak it held a ring. There was a sudden fluttering and the other magpie swooped in front of me and settled on the picture rail on the right hand wall. The bird rearranged its wings and turned so that its long tail was clear of the frame of the nearest picture. The brass it held in its beak clattered to the floor. As it fell it knocked a picture frame slightly out of line. I looked at the painting and saw the ghostly lines of the oak branches fading away as though into a dream. There was a mist over the branches. I raised the torch and aimed straight at the frame. When the light clicked on and struck the branches there was a great beating of wings, a buffeting of all the air in the room, the brushing of startled wings across my face and the two birds melted back into their positions in the wonderful painting.

I said that I did not expect you to believe the story. I knew it was hopeless to explain it to my father; I tried the next day but he would not believe any of it . . . until I took the picture down and all the missing trinkets showered noisily on to the carpet.

CELANDINE AND PERIWINKLE

A COLD, MOONLIT EVENING. The 11th February 1966. My 22nd birthday.

Miss Evans had invited me to her room to have a glass of port. She was only in her sixties, but to me, a young man, she seemed like rather an old lady. She was a bonny white-haired spinster who'd been the headmaster's secretary for thirty years.

I told her I wasn't sure I should have a glass of port. I was taking a group of boys into the woods at seven o'clock, to listen for the owl and search for pellets.

'I know,' she said. 'But one glass won't hurt. It'll keep you warm out there.'

Before I could ask her how she knew, she said, 'Mr Bunce told me. He's pleased, in his usual gruff and grumpy sort of way, that you're setting up your own little club, however odd it might be. He thinks it's important that every teacher in the school has a special niche of his own, whether it's sports or art or music or drama, or a hobby like stamps or brass-rubbing or ... well, even something a bit odd like your owls and collecting their pellets.'

She filled up two large glasses. 'Tawny port. Good luck with the owls.'

Her living-room, which overlooked the stable-yard where I'd arranged to meet my boys in half an hour or so, was an airless fug. The single bar of her electric heater was buzzing and fizzing white-hot. Her dog, a pug with a horribly wrinkled black face, was snoring on the rug.

'Cheers,' she said, 'and happy birthday. Drink up. I can give you a mint to suck before you go out. Oh, and I've got something else for you . . .'

It was another owl-joke, along with the tawny port. She reached to the floor beside her armchair and picked up a box of chocolates. 'Have one of these. And give them to your boys . . . what do you think?'

We laughed together as I opened the chocolates. They were dark, almost black, each one about an inch long and studded with fragments of walnut. Miss Evans peered closely at the box and intoned in very English-sounding French, '*Biscuits à la noisette, couverts de chocolat noir* . . . what do they look like to you?'

The same size and shape and colour as the ones we would find under the old oak tree. Deliciously edible, chocolate owl pellets.

And the port was lovely, rich and sweet. I thought I heard boys' voices and their footsteps outside in the yard, but as soon as I started fidgeting to get up and look out of the window Miss Evans clucked at me to sit down and relax. By the time I'd reached for another chocolate she'd refilled my glass.

'They'll be all right for another five minutes, don't worry. They can't get lost in the stable-yard. Of course, out in the deep dark dangerous forest it's a different thing altogether . . .'

A bit odd, yes. I'd gone to talk about it to Mr Bunce in his study the previous week. He was a tall, sinewy man in his fifties, a classicist, with a Welsh accent. He wore tiny round glasses, and he had a hearing-aid in

his left ear, which he fiddled with, fuming, whenever it
started to whistle. He reminded me of an aphorism I'd
read somewhere – that he had all the characteristics of a
poker, except for its occasional warmth. But I thought,
maybe one day, if I stayed long enough at the school, I
might discover a glimmer of mischief in him.

He'd hired me in September as a young, willing kind
of dogsbody teacher, straight out of university with my
gentleman's degree, to do English and French and even
a bit of Latin for a couple of terms or a year and see how
I got on. At the start of my second term, in January, he'd
taken me aside in the staffroom and suggested it was
time for me to take charge of something, anything at all,
to make a contribution to the life of the school beyond
my normal teaching. When, a few days later, I went into
his study and he took off his glasses and leaned back in
his chair to hear what I'd come up with, I supposed he
was hoping I'd offer to coach rugby to the 2nd XV or
maybe help Mr Pym to organize the inter-house debating competition. He cocked his head as though he was
listening to me carefully, although he didn't invite me
to sit down. Then, when I'd finished, he stared at me in
silence for a very long minute.

I was beginning to think he hadn't heard a word I'd
said. But at last he said, very softly and slowly, 'Owls . . .
pellets . . . owl pellets.' He closed his eyes. 'The regurgitated undigested remains of mice and voles and
shrews . . .'

He blinked his eyes open and stared at me for another
silent minute. And then he sighed and put his glasses
back onto his nose and waved me out of the room.

'Yes, yes, that will do . . . only remember . . .' and I'd
swerved back to the door to catch what he was about

to say, 'remember what a serious responsibility it is, to take charge of other people's children and keep them safely supervised at all times, even when you're . . . even when you're just rummaging around for . . . for owl pellets . . .'

Now, on my 22nd birthday, dear old Miss Evans was snoring. Just like her dog, she'd closed her eyes and her mouth was wide open, and I had to jump up quickly to catch her glass of port before she dropped it onto the carpet.

I drained my own glass and hers too. Feeling a glow of comfortable contentment through my throat and into my chest, I warmed the backs of my legs in front of her buzzing fire. And then I picked up my birthday chocolates, let myself out and went downstairs to the stable-yard . . .

*

Where the boys played a little trick on me, as seven- and eight-year olds do with a young, inexperienced teacher.

They must have heard my footsteps clattering down the steps from Miss Evans' room, as I'd hurried past the music room and paused in the changing-room to grab my coat . . . and they'd all hidden, holding their breath, in the darkest shadows of the yard.

Bright moonlight, a half-moon in a cloudless sky, and pitch-black shadows . . . I was alone in the silence.

I knew they were there. I played along. As I put on my coat and pulled the collar up to my ears, I let my shadow assume an enormous, hunched, billowing shape . . . ghoulish and immensely terrifying, except that it was only Mr Drew, who was new at the school and making a hesitant, slightly dithering start to his life as a teacher. The boys let me do this for a few more moments, as I readjusted my coat and saw my shadow shrink and shift and shimmy, as I pretended to peer around me. They let me huff and puff and mutter a bit before they sprang out to surprise me, hissing like demons.

'All right, all right . . . calm down . . . are we all here?'

They ignored me, pushing and shoving together. There would be five of them . . . Stuttaford, Beale, Henderson, Fletcher and Tetley. I'd suggested the outing at the end of their Latin class in the morning, and the five of them had volunteered straightaway. I guessed it was just for the novelty of it really, something different to be doing between prep and bedtime on a winter's night instead of playing table-tennis or chess or mooching in the dorm . . . for four of them at least. But I knew that Tetley was genuinely intrigued.

Tetley had shown an interest as soon as I'd set up a nature table at the back of my classroom, with the owl pellets I'd already found in the woods. I was glad he'd had the nerve to put up his hand. He was the quietest, shyest boy in the class, unusually small, even for a seven-year-old, and different. Expected to be musical, because his father was a concert pianist making a reputation for himself in London and Paris and Berlin, he'd been delivered to the school with his own cello, an expensive instrument almost as big as him, in a fat black fur-lined case with brass fasteners.

Poor little Tetley . . . different, yes. He was a pasty little loner, an easy target for the other boys. He must have wished, sometimes, that he could have taken out the ridiculous cello and hidden inside the case himself.

The senior master Mr Pym had asked me to keep an eye on him, in case he was bullied or teased. So I was pleased whenever the boy stayed behind in break-time, to avoid the rough and tumble of the playground, and he helped me to dissect some of the pellets and display the contents onto sheets of blotting paper. He labelled them with his big loopy handwriting: the skull of a shrew, the bones of a wren, the chitinous fragments of beetles gleaming like splinters of jet.

He'd asked if he could keep some of the pellets, and when I'd said yes he put a few of them into his pocket.

Now, in the stable-yard, the boys dashed around me, as though my shadow had smashed into smithereens and shattered in the moonlight. And I was saying, 'All right, all right, let's go . . .' all strict and schoolmasterly, 'Come on, come on . . .'

I marched ahead of them. I felt the warmth of the port suffusing my body. The boys formed a single pool of shadow. They were chattering and giggling, excited to be outside in the cold February night . . . until we'd gone a hundred yards away from the school and reached the edge of the woodland. They fell into a breathless, shivering silence.

*

Bright moonlight? Strange . . . as soon as we entered the woodland, the air became clammy and dull. We came to the lake. The still black water was exhaling a kind of mist, which rose into the branches of the trees and clung there.

A couple of the boys – Stuttaford and Fletcher I

thought – were whispering together and trying to put
on a bit of bravado. A sudden sound . . . we all stopped
and listened, there was a moment when all of us, even
me, felt a prickle of fear in our scalps . . . a loud splash in
the lake, as though something quite big had risen from
the depths and broken the surface. Or else something
had fallen into the water, maybe a branch from an over-
hanging tree.

I turned and glared at Stuttaford, who had lingered
a few paces behind the rest of the group, thinking he
might have thrown something into the water to make
us all stop and stare. But he only shrugged and took a
step or two forward. His separate shape rejoined the
grey-black shadow of coats and scarves which was all I
could see of the other boys.

We trudged deeper into the forest. Darker and colder.
No moon. A lowering white fog.

At last we reached the old oak tree on the further side
of the lake. I'd been there earlier in the afternoon, in
glorious, unseasonably warm sunshine. Preparing for
the night-time expedition, I'd strolled into the woods
with a pocketful of owl pellets I'd borrowed from the
nature table in my classroom. Lovely, to see the celandine gleaming golden, to kneel and push aside the
early spring grasses to find periwinkle and the tiny,
exquisite flowers of the nettle. The robin was singing,
the wren was in full-throated, full-bodied song . . . and
everywhere among the bare trees there was a shower of
willow catkins. I'd gone to the oak tree, where I knew
the tawny owl perched at night and digested, or partly
digested, his prey, and I'd found a half-dozen of his pellets in the leaf litter at the base of the trunk . . . for good
measure I'd scattered a few more, to make sure that the

boys would all find something later in the evening, how-ever dim and dark the woods might be.

Dim and dark. And cold. We stopped in the bone-chilling darkness.

I told the boys to hurry and look for the pellets. There might be a prize, I told them, or some prizes, if they found anything. One of them, Tetley I supposed it was, as the keenest member of the group, was kneeling on the ground and feeling among the long, twisted roots of the tree. It gave me a moment to move away and uri-nate discreetly ... or as discreetly as I could, because the world was such a still, silent place that the sound and steam I created were impossible to disguise.

Silent. If, that night, there were owls in the woodland, not one was making a sound ... not a long quavering, querying hoot or a quick-quick response.

Shivering, I felt a dull ache between my shoulder blades. The warm glow of two and a half glasses of tawny port had long gone. But, as I pushed my hands deep into my pockets, I felt the six chocolates that Miss Evans had suggested I bring with me. And, in the mist of the trees and the chill breath of the lake, they brought back to me the small, reassuringly cumulative moments of happiness I'd enjoyed on my 22nd birthday ... nice lessons in the morning ... the nervous anticipation of this expedition with the boys ... my own walk in the afternoon ... a surreptitious drink with Miss Evans and her casual disclosure that I'd won the approval of Mr Bunce. A good day, so far ...

The boys gathered around me. They wanted to show me what they'd found. Fumbling in the gloom, I quickly gave out the prizes, and they made gruesome gagging noises as they got the joke and ate the chocolates, pretending to mix them up with the real owl pellets they'd found.

I ate a chocolate too. Sweet and bitter and delicious, it reminded my taste-buds of the port I'd enjoyed in Miss Evans' overheated room. Yes, a good day . . . but it was time to get moving and back to the relative warmth and comfort of school.

The boys handed me their pellets, to take back for the nature table. I was about to drop them into the pocket of my coat, when I found I still had one chocolate left.

I asked the boys if they'd all had one. 'Stuttaford? Beale? Henderson? Fletcher?' They all said yes. 'Tetley? Where's Tetley?'

No answer. I said it again. 'Tetley? Are you there?'

Stuttaford said, 'No, sir. He isn't here, sir.'

I said, 'What do you mean, he isn't here? Where is he?'

Stuttaford said, 'I don't know, sir. I mean, we don't know.'

*

I counted the boys. One, two, three, four. I counted them again, twice and a third time and a fourth time, touching each boy on the top of his head. One, two, three, four . . . as though it might somehow, magically, conjure a fifth boy.

'But he was here . . .' I blustered at them, 'I mean, Tetley was there, in the yard . . . wasn't he? When I came downstairs? When we set off from the school . . . he was in the yard, wasn't he?'

The four boys muttered back at me and to each other. 'Not sure, sir. We're not sure. Yes, he might've been . . .

I think he was. Yes, he was. Wasn't he? No, I don't think . . .'

We turned and stumbled through the woods. I called out the name, not so loudly, not really shouting, because the word echoed so foolishly in such an otherworldly place . . . the woodland in winter, at night, a world in which such a word as 'Tetley' . . . uttered either with a falling intonation, as though a command, or with an upward lilt, like an absurd question . . . sounded ridiculous.

We came to the lake. I was breathing hard. My mouth was sticky, the after-taste of the chocolate was annoying, it was irrelevant, it had nothing to do with what was happening now, out in the woods. I stared across the water. The surface was grey and still and smothered in mist, and the memory of the sudden splash we'd all heard was appalling. I made sure the remaining four boys were gathered close and completely silent, and I called the name . . . 'Tetley!' first as a command, as though to order his reappearance, and then 'Tetley?' to question where on earth he'd gone.

Not a sound. A terrible, suffocating silence. If one of the other boys, probably Stuttaford, had thought it was funny to throw something into the water and startle us all, he didn't dare do it again now. My mouth was dry. My skin was cold with a deadly cold sweat. We hurried past the lake and out of the woodland. We left behind the fog which had clung to us and shrouded the moon, and the world was bright and silvery as we ran back towards the school.

*

Mr Bunce was in the stable-yard. Tall and angular in a duffel coat and scarf, he was dancing. Or rather, he was doing what I'd been doing about an hour ago, enjoying the moonlight, assuming poses and throwing his own shadows. We surprised him, our prickly headmaster, in a childish private moment . . . and when he heard our footsteps he froze in an oddly statuesque pose and fixed an awkward little half-smile onto his face.

'Ah, Mr Drew.' He pulled himself straight. 'I thought I might come out and wait for you. It's such a lovely night . . .'

We stopped in front of him. He frowned, seeing me so breathless and tousled. 'Well, Mr Drew, is everything all right? What's the matter? No owls? No pellets?'

He saw that I could hardly breathe, let alone answer his query about the owls. He ran an experienced teacher's eye over the boys, saw how they ducked away and hid behind me, and he said sharply, 'Well, Stuttaford? Beale? Speak up. Didn't you find anything?'

No answer. I had almost recovered myself, although my muddled, panic-stricken brain hadn't decided what I was going to say, when he went on, 'What about Tetley? Where are you, Tetley? I hope you've come back with a pocketful of pellets for Mr Drew's nature table . . .'

'No sir, no Mr Bunce . . .' I started to say. 'I mean yes, yes, we've got plenty of pellets. But no Tetley . . .'

'No Tetley? What do you mean? Speak up. Where is he?'

There was a dead silence. Mr Bunce fumbled at his hearing-aid. The boy Stuttaford said what I couldn't say. 'Tetley's not here, sir. We don't know where he is.'

*

The headmaster ushered the four boys indoors, to go immediately to their dormitories and get ready for bed.

A minute later, I was following him up and up the stairs and along the corridors. In Tetley's dorm we found his bed still neatly made up since the morning and no sign of the boy . . . and Miss Hayes, the school nurse, flustered and red-faced in the unexpected presence of the headmaster, was saying of course Tetley wasn't there, the boy had had permission to be out late with Mr Drew. She fumbled into the pocket of her nurse's tunic, between her left breast and her upside-down watch, and found the slip of paper I'd written for her, saying that the boy Tetley would be in the woods with me until nine o'clock . . . and she stammered, even more red-faced, as she read out loud that he would be 'l-l-l-listening for owls and looking for their p-p-pellets'.

Mr Deuce appeared, the master on duty in the dormitories that night. He confirmed that Tetley was officially absent and accounted for. He gestured at the made-up bed as though it was the answer we were looking for . . . Tetley had permission to be elsewhere, he was elsewhere, so what was the problem?

There was a problem. A boy was missing.

And so began a long night of barely controlled panic and fear inside and around the school. Mr Deuce was ordered to get the boys into bed and their lights switched off as quickly as possible and to stay in the house with them. The word quickly went round the school, to every annexe and apartment and study and classroom, for all the other resident teachers and staff to gather for an emergency meeting outside the headmaster's study.

And so they came, from in front of their televisions, from their pipes and their sherry and their drowsy bach-

elor daydreams, a rather befuddled group of middle-
aged prep-school teachers.

A boy was missing. A boy was lost. Tetley. He'd been
out with Mr Drew.

Out? Yes, out. Out in the woods. Or maybe not.
Maybe he was still in the school.

Mr Drew, me . . . I was gulping and blinking in front
of fifteen uncomprehending members of the staff. No,
I couldn't confirm whether Tetley had been with me or
not when we'd left the stable yard.

There was a volley of questions. Owls? Owl pellets?
Why? What for? How many boys? Five? Four? You don't
know? What do you mean, you don't know? Didn't
you count them, didn't you have a list, didn't you tick
off their names, do a roll-call? You didn't? Why not? So
where is Tetley? In the school? Or is he somewhere out
there, in the woods?

This last question . . . well, it was the last question.
The silence which followed it was so cold, so huge, so
terrifying, that the only ensuing sounds were a shuffling of slippers and indoor shoes and the whistle of Mr
Bunce's hearing-aid. He himself looked suddenly frail, a
few dried-up sticks of a man . . . and so the senior master,
the reassuringly large and long-serving and dependable
Mr Pym, stepped up and took control. Within another
minute, he'd organized different groups of teachers to
search different areas. And the search began.

Miss Evans . . . she'd appeared at the end of the meeting. I'd heard her footsteps along the corridor and the
laboured breathing of her pug. She looked anything
but bonny. She must have answered a sudden rapping
on her door and she'd been asleep, wrapped up in her
dressing-gown in front of the electric fire. Her face was

mottled and oddly misshapen, on her right cheek there
was a wrinkled map of her sleep, the imprinted material
of her armchair. She'd arrived in time to get the urgency
of what was happening, to sense the anxiety and even
the unspoken panic in the extraordinary meeting.
When she saw me standing alone and dazed, when all
the others had hurried away, she came closer to me . . .
so close that I could smell the staleness of the port on
her breath.

'They'll find him,' she whispered. 'Or maybe you'll
find him yourself.'

She pressed something into my hand. A mint. She
shuffled away.

*

With the mint in my mouth, as hard as a pebble and
clacking against my teeth, I tried to help. I would do
anything to help. To try and clear away the smother-
ing of fear which was preventing me from thinking or
remembering or recalling the events of the past hour or
so, I tried to join this group or that group of teachers in
their search. Each one seemed to blank me away. They
didn't want me. I wasn't one of them, I wasn't a proper
teacher, serious and responsible and seasoned by years
of experience. I was a silly young man. No common
sense. No gumption.

I found myself out in the stable-yard, where our
expedition had started so promisingly, in a dazzle of
moonlight, in a haze of port. I stood exactly where I'd
been standing when the boys had burst out of the shadows, and I squeezed my eyes shut and tried to count
them. Were there five of them, or only four? But it was

impossible, it had been impossible, as they'd wriggled
and hissed and tussled around me.

I followed our footsteps, away from the school and
to the edge of the woodland. Ahead of me everywhere,
I saw the flashlights of the teachers as they searched
among the trees. I heard their voices and the repetition
of that word . . . Tetley! . . . as a peremptory command,
the kind of stern and serious voice that the hapless
young Mr Drew was incapable of mustering . . . and
Tetley? . . . a hopeful entreaty which rang and echoed
and waited for a reply which didn't come.

Lights and voices, like some kind of game these
stern and serious grown-ups were playing in the wintry
woods, or a piece of theatre they were enacting . . .

I caught up with some of them, and watched,
stricken with horror at the ghastliness of what they
were doing. Shushing one another, thinking they had
found something, some thing, they were pointing their
torches into a hole, maybe a badger's set or the den of
a fox, and they were kneeling and scrabbling and trying
to tug something out of it. One of the men actually
thrust his head and shoulders into the hole . . . there was
a horrid muttering of expectation . . . until at last, with
a ghastly wrench and a snapping like breaking bones, he
fell out backwards with nothing but a branch or a root
he had pulled out. He lay on the ground, heaving for
breath, and then, as they all struggled to their feet again
with the torches white on their fearful faces, they saw
me standing and watching . . . and the coldness of their
exasperation sent me stumbling away.

Another group I happened upon, deeper in the
woods . . . and it was even worse, in the absurdity of
what they were doing.

Someone had glimpsed something, high in the trees. Absurd, and yet even more horrifying in its absurdity . . . for yes, when they flashed their torchlights up and up into the bare branches, yes there was a dark shape, and it was moving, it was swaying and it was dangling there, it was hanging. More manly muttering and murmuring . . . what was it, whatever could it be? . . . until one of the men, a strong athletic man who was strict and stern and admired for the discipline he wielded in his classroom, he swarmed up the tree and reached the thing we all dreaded he might find . . . and he tore at it, spluttering and swearing with the sheer frustration of what he was doing, and tossed down nothing but a great clump of mistletoe.

And at the lake? The awfulness of it. The futile heroics. Some of the men, two or three of them, were actually wading in the shallows, and then up to their waists . . . and calling out the boy's name and clapping their hands and even slapping at the water, as though they might . . . if in their worst nightmare the boy was in there . . . they might arouse him and bring him gasping and gagging to the surface. For they guessed that Mr Drew and his four of five boys must have passed by the lake on their ridiculous outing, they knew from their shouted communications with the other groups of searchers that they'd been tunneling into the ground and even climbing the trees, so they had to match them in their brave futility . . . to do their duty by engaging with the lake, by entering the deadly black water.

I watched them, a useless spectator. They reached across the water, where someone had seen something glistening and bobbing on the surface. Their hands found cold white skin. They cried out, with fear and

revulsion as their fingers slipped and struggled to grip,
and they pulled. In a welter of torch-beams, they waded
to the edge of the lake and dragged a body ashore. A
sheep or maybe a deer, bloated and nude after weeks in
the water.

*

Tetley? Where was he? A little boy, seven years old . . .
frail and pale and very lonely . . . whose parents had
driven him to a country prep-school a hundred miles
away from home, delivered him into the care of a lot
of complete strangers and then driven away . . . and for
good measure, had cursed him with a notion that he
might be musical and should be taught to play the cello.
Poor little Tetley.

Now, thanks to me and unbeknown to his parents,
those strangers were looking for him in the oddest of
places. Tetley, who should have been at home with his
mother and father, watching the television with them
in their living-room with a glass of milk and a chocolate biscuit before going to bed in his own bedroom . . .
where was he? Up a tree? In a hole? In a lake?

I found myself . . . an hour before I found Tetley . . .
back in the stable-yard.

If the boy wasn't in the woods he must be in the
school. It struck me, too late, that he wasn't the kind
of boy to have joined in with the others' prank, hiding
in the shadows and then hurtling out like banshees.
I should have known, back then, that Tetley was too
timid to have joined in with those hissing, chattering
shadows. And I cursed myself, my well-meaning naïve
self, for unwittingly adding to the boy's oddity and the

likelihood of his being picked on. Poor boy. He was already lumbered with the grand and self-important cello, while he was so pale and meek... and then, in charge of my nature table, he'd assumed a ridiculous role as Mr Drew's swotty little pet with a pocketful of owl pellets.

I turned back into the changing rooms, hoping I would find his coat still hanging there. It wasn't. I pushed open the door of the music room and peered into the darkness. The precious cello was propped into a corner, I saw the gleam of the strings and the shapely curves of its body, and the case lying on the floor.

I paused at the stairs up to Miss Evans' room, wondering how she was passing these anxious hours. Had she fallen asleep again in front of her fire, or was she wide-awake and pondering her part in it all, that she'd been complicit in young Mr Drew's carelessness by plying him with port before he took the boys into the woods? The mint, I remembered the mint, she'd sought me out and proffered the mint... not because she was concerned for me and to shield me from even more blame for my irresponsibility, but to cover herself. Dear old Miss Evans, skulking upstairs in her room and hoping that her reputation would remain intact.

To my classroom. It was moonlit. I edged between the rows of desks to the nature table. The pellets, and the remains of the beasts and birds and beetles which had been compacted inside them, had been crumbled and strewn about. Tetley's neatly handwritten labels were scattered on the floor.

Softly upstairs. I heard Mr Deuce's footsteps along the corridor, for he was doing his duty as seriously as all his colleagues in the woods... solely and solemnly responsible for all of the remaining boys, he was patrolling from dorm to dorm. For sure, as much as the other teachers were striving to find the one missing boy, Mr Deuce was committed to the safety of all the rest.

I tiptoed behind him. Once, he stopped and turned and stared back into the darkness . . . and I ducked into a doorway and held my breath until my chest was hurting. When he moved on, I moved into the dormitory and stood there, in silence.

Tetley's empty bed. In the other beds, their faces silvery in a shaft of moonlight, the boys were asleep.

No, not all of them. There were four other beds empty. Unaware that I had entered the room . . . perhaps they'd waited until Mr Deuce's footsteps had receded and they'd thought he was the only teacher in the house . . . four boys were standing at the window. In their pyjamas, perfectly still and breathless, they were watching the flickering of torchlight in the woods.

Stuttaford? Beale and Henderson and Fletcher? From the shadows of the doorway I watched what they were watching. It was lovely, and it was terrifying. A host of fireflies, breathtaking in their ephemeral beauty? No. A search-party of schoolteachers, exhausted, despairing, stumbling and swearing in the forest, fearing that a small boy who was lost might never be found . . .

I took a breath, to whisper in the big cold room. Do you know where he is? Tell me, if you know where he is . . .

But the words lay mute on my tongue. Before I could break the unearthly silence, the four boys turned away from the window. With a shiver and a rustle of sheets, they seemed to melt back into their beds.

Not a sound. And yet I heard something, a voice in

my head, not answering the question but prompting me to a sudden clarity of thought.

They'll find him. Or perhaps you'll find him yourself . . .

And it came to me. I knew where he was. I would find him because I knew where he was. I'd imagined already where he might be.

In less than a minute I'd clattered down the stairs. I didn't care that I would wake the boys or arouse the attention of the vigilant Mr Deuce. Down the stairs and skidding past the foot of Miss Evans' stairs, past the changing room . . . and pushing open the door of the music room.

The cello. So expensive, so precious. Propped into a corner.

The fur-lined case, on the floor. A scatter of dark and dusty crumbs all around it, a few of the fragments glittering like jet. I knelt and struggled to undo the big brass fasteners and I opened the case. Tetley was inside it.

*

All credit to Miss Evans. In my anxiety and self-recrimination, I'd cast around in my mind for anyone to blame as much as myself. And I'd hit on Miss Evans and her copious measures of port and then the mint, as though she and I were equally responsible for the loss of Tetley . . . for the loss of a seven-year-old boy who might never be found . . . or found dead in a badger's set or hanging in a tree or floating in a dark cold lake.

He was curled inside the cello case, his legs pulled up to his chest. His eyes were closed. His face was very white. But he was breathing. As soon as I opened the case, he opened his eyes. I touched his cheek. He looked at me, with a tiny crooked smile on his mouth as though he was glad I'd found him . . . then he struggled to sit up, and he vomited feebly onto my hands.

I ran for Miss Evans. She hurried downstairs in her dressing-gown and slippers. She sat on the floor, as tender and loving as a grandma, and cuddled the boy and gave him water to drink and to bathe his face. He was warm and alive. He wouldn't speak. He only wanted to fold himself into the arms and the warm bonny body of Miss Evans. The three of us were sitting together on the floor of the music room, when Mr Pym came back into the house and found us. And the search was over.

*

Celandine, periwinkle . . . another glorious afternoon, the day after my 22nd birthday.

The robin, deceived into lovely, silvery, springtime song by the warm sunshine of late February. The wren, a little brown trog with a belting voice, nothing less than a miracle.

I was walking through the woods. Mr Bunce had suggested it, past the lake and the old oak tree and onwards and the path would emerge by the road. A bus would come along and I could choose to go into town and take a train and go home . . . have a long weekend or a week off . . . or choose to leave for good and never come back and try something else.

He'd given me the choice. He and Mr Pym. They'd found something good in me, they'd said, that I was kind and willing and well-meaning and who knows, I might make a teacher one day. Mr Bunce, with a glimmer of mischief behind his icy little glasses and a sidelong glance at Mr Pym, had said there was more to being a good schoolmaster than rugger and even debating... although night-time walks into the woods mightn't be resumed for a while.

As for Tetley, Mr Bunce had called his parents. Once the boy had been found alive and well, or at least reasonably composed and responsive to a warm bath and a change of clothes and a bit of breakfast, the headmaster might have opted for a lull and an agreement in a staff meeting that the matter was closed and no one need say anything. But no. The night had been too awful. Everyone had been so frightened, they'd done oddly heroic deeds in the woods, things they would remember forever and through all the days of their careers as teachers, that it couldn't be forgotten. Mr Bunce had summoned me into his study. He'd told me he'd talked to Mr Pym and some of the other teachers, who, this morning, were still bruised and shaken and chilled from their exertions in the night, and he'd really had no choice but to call Tetley's parents.

So Mr and Mrs Tetley came to take their little boy home, not forgetting, of course, the precious cello. Miss Hayes had cleaned out the case, where the boy had vomited. In his study ... with reassuring Mr Pym and sweet Miss Evans, and with me as the teacher who'd found the boy and restored him to his present well-being ... Mr Bunce informed the parents that their son had been rather unhappy at the school, that possibly a few of the bigger boys had teased him about the cello, although young Mr Drew had tried to keep an eye out for him and had actively involved him in his nature studies ... and the boy had worried the staff last night by going missing for an hour or two and had eventually been found, snug and warm, inside the case of his cello.

I'd said yes yes, when Mr Bunce had paused and glanced across at me to confirm what he'd said.

The previous day, my birthday? That long and terrible night? No, I erased all of that. For a ghastly split-second I thought of a phrase I'd heard in my head . . . unbeknown to the parents. And I knew they would never know about the horrible madness . . . of their son, lost in the woods. Up a tree? in a hole? in the lake? lost forever? dead?

So what did I say? I said I'd been concerned since the beginning of the January term that little Tetley . . . amazing, that none of us, apart from possibly Miss Evans, who kept the details of all the boys in her immaculate files, none of us knew this seven-year-old boy's first name . . . I said I'd been concerned that the boy might be homesick. When he'd gone missing and we'd looked everywhere for him, I'd had a brainwave, seeing that such an expensive cello was leaning in a corner in the music room and wasn't in its case . . . and I'd opened the case and found the boy hiding.

I emerged from the woods and came to the road.

Bright sunlight. Celandine and periwinkle. The bus came, and as it approached and slowed down I got ready to step onboard. I felt in my pocket, for some change to give to the driver . . .

But then I changed my mind and waved for the bus to go by. I walked back through the woods, towards the school. In my pocket, a crumble of owl pellets . . . the undigested, regurgitated remains of mice and voles and shrews. And a left-over chocolate biscuit.

THE CORMORANT

THE SAMPHIRE was the only pub in the village. It was owned and run by Harry Luff and his wife, Rachel. They had been there for 17 years. In the summer months when holidaymakers came to the coast business was good. But in the winter, when the village was shaken by the big tides, chafed by the sand and salt, The Samphire was quiet. Only a few gloomy locals came to drink—shopkeepers, schoolteachers and fishermen foiled by the weather.

It was September, the end of the summer season. Harry Luff had entertained his visitors for the past three or four months with his easy humour, his big voice. The trippers liked Harry. He was something of a dandy, favouring the bright waistcoat and bowtie. There was a twinkle in his eyes and his bald head was highly polished. Rachel smiled to herself and said little. She was tiny, with dry blond hair and a chalky complexion. She was content to leave the banter to her husband, while she busied herself behind the bar, scurrying back and forth like a laboratory mouse.

Then Harry broke his thumb. It was smashed by a wayward rolling barrel in the cellar under the pub. At the cottage hospital the thumb was set with a steel pin inside it. A heavy plaster cast covered his whole hand and his forearm. He was in pain from the moment the barrel shattered his thumb, and for weeks after the operation. But there was no longer the white electric agony of the first contact. It was as though the pin in his hand contained some secret energy of its own, because it pulsed and throbbed, sending waves of aching heat up and down Harry's arm. He could do nothing behind the bar of The Samphire. A lad was hired to help Rachel with the heavy work of changing barrels and so on, while Harry sat out front with the customers and rested his heavy cast on the bar.

It was the end of the season anyway, so The Samphire was not busy. Harry spent the hours when the pub was open leaning on the bar and drinking with the locals. Rachel worked. As she worked, a glow came over her white face, but still she smiled to herself. Harry said little. The pain came and went up to his elbow and he eased it with more drinking. He was irritable. The pin in his thumb sent out its pounding messages, blanking out Harry's humour and replacing it with a sort of morose tension. Between spasms of pain he waited. When they came, his lips went pale. There seemed to be fewer and fewer customers in The Samphire. Harry inflicted his pain on them, so they drank quickly and left.

Harry and Rachel quarrelled. Or rather, Harry shouted and breathed whisky over Rachel. She continued with her work, holding a glass up to the light to see that it was clean. Through the glass, the tiny pearls of moisture on her forehead were magnified. A few strands of blond hair stuck to her temples. The customers looked away, embarrassed, so that Harry was ashamed and stalked out of the pub, across the road to the seafront. He tramped along the beaches, his feet crunching into the pebbles. The pain remained. It was not uncommon to find Rachel alone behind the bar in the afternoons, while Harry stumbled over the seaweed-slippery boulders at the foot of the cliffs.

At the end of September Harry came back from the beach with a bird. It was a young cormorant. Its breast and left wing were fouled with oil. In the falling gloom of late afternoon Harry had found it lying helpless in a tidal pool. His head had cleared enough for him to see it and pity it, wrap it in his thick pullover and carry it back to The Samphire. Before the pub opened at six o'clock, he had cleaned the cormorant with a little detergent and wrapped it again in some old curtains. The first customers were surprised by the sight of the sinuous neck and dangerous-looking beak which rose from the thick material. Harry put it on the bar. The bird blinked sometimes, it moved its head slowly from side to side. It opened its beak and panted—fish-breath, eel-breath, the smell of the beach. Within a few days it was strong enough to stand on the bar without its wrappings of curtains and blankets.

Rachel loathed the cormorant for its bad manners. Harry fed it with cat food and laughed when its neck convulsed, its murderous beak opened wide, and the mess was vomited up on to the bar. But the bird thrived. The feathers became thick and shiny. The raw patches of bare skin around its nostrils were soon covered in a carpet of moleskin down. The cormorant seemed glad to stay in the smoky confines of The Samphire's bar, pattering up and down on its wide feet. Sometimes it squirted excrement on to the polished woodwork, raising its tough tail feathers and aiming mischievously. Harry laughed, forgetting the pain in his thumb. Rachel was exasperated; she wrinkled her little nose in disgust as she cleared up the mess. The customers liked the show and the bird became something of a celebrity. Harry and Rachel still quarrelled, and Harry took himself out on to the beach. But he quickly came back to feed his bird.

It was the plaster cast that fascinated the young cormorant. As Harry sat on a tall stool with his damaged hand on the bar, the bird would sidle along suspiciously, eyeing the dirty white plaster and snaking its long neck. Then it began to peck gently and nibble until the bar around its feet was sprinkled with the crumbs of plaster. The cormorant swallowed nothing. It was the texture of the dry chalky cast which attracted it, not the taste. There was something about the powdery stuff which brought it each time slapping its webbed feet along the polished bar to tap-tap-tap at the cast. Harry was delighted. Soon his cast was pocked with the light blows from the cormorant's beak. Rachel frowned and swept away the powder with her duster.

Either Harry became accustomed to the pain from the pin in his thumb or the pain decreased, because he began to resume his normal role of raconteur and jovial host in The Samphire. Perhaps he was distracted by the attentions of the cormorant. Still it retched into the ashtrays and held out its wings as though for the applause of the customers. It snaked its long neck. It practised its guttural cries until it became quite accomplished in its reproduction of a polite cough, as though it was a butler embarrassed by his master's tactlessness. Harry laughed at the bird and the fishermen laughed as well. Only Rachel pursed her lips when the cormorant raised its tail suddenly, to lower it again without disgracing itself. The bird seemed to love the guffaws which greeted these false alarms—then it was so much funnier when

the moment came to aim its yellow squirt and relish the
cheers of the customers. To Rachel they were children,
and Harry was a silly boor. But business was better for
the bird's presence. Harry's plaster was chipped away
bit by bit. Winter settled around the village as the seas
pounded the coast, the mists rolled in, big gulls were
forced to shelter among the chimney pots, and sandbags
were got ready at the doorways of the seafront cottages.

Harry, who was still no use behind the bar, continued
to drink. He maintained that his injury prevented him
from helping Rachel with even the lightest tasks. So he
sat with the cormorant, put it through its tricks for the
benefit of his friends, and drank with them. The plaster was wearing thin in places. Harry moved his hand
round slowly so that the wear from the bird's increas-
ingly powerful beak was even. Perhaps it was attracted
by the throbbing energy of the steel pin. Still Harry
suffered an occasional lancing pain, and the cormorant
nibbled away as though hypnotized by the hidden steel.
But the heat generated in Harry's stomach by the doses
of whisky, and the heat kindled in the eye of the cormorant by the thought of the pin in its master's thumb . . .
these grew just as the ice formed inside the sickened
soul of Rachel Luff. She felt it forming. No one else in
The Samphire had sensed it. But it was there—for the
fools in the bar, for Harry and for the cormorant.

As the ice formed, so it grew in weight; it was inevitable that soon, like heavy icicles above a well used pave-
ment, it would crack and fall. One stormy afternoon a
handful of customers were blown into The Samphire.
The rain lashed the windows. The waves struck the seafront and fired their bullets of spray across the promenade. Inside the pub the cormorant was restless. It

yawned, it coughed, it held out its wings and beat them, like an old parson shaking the dust from his gown. It wriggled its neck. When Harry drummed his fingers on the bar, the bird waddled towards him and began to peck at the remains of the plaster cast. Harry bought the drinks, and there was laughter. The windows of the pub steamed up with the slow drying of overcoats. Rachel performed her duties mechanically, loaded with ice. She felt it shift inside her. It was too much.

So, when the bird brought up its gulletful of cat food and potato crisps on to the bar in front of her, when it shot a stream of slime all over her carefully hand-written menu, Rachel had had enough. The storm of laughter stopped in mid-guffaw as she shot out her slender arm and closed her hand like a vice around the cormorant's throat. The customers in The Samphire and its landlord were too stunned by Rachel's attack to move or speak. With the bird croaking and choking and battering its wings, coughing and convulsing in her grip, Rachel strode to the door, opened it so the rain was suddenly blown into her face, and hurled the wretched cormorant out into the street. She slammed the door shut. When she turned to the men in the room, her white face was quivering with triumph. The hard smile which set on her lips remained even when her husband lurched towards her, shoved her aside and disappeared through the door into the rain.

Harry's friends shuffled out in silence, cowed by the freezing glances which Rachel shot at them from the doorway. There were little drops of rain on her face and on her eyelashes. Then she was alone in The Samphire. In a few minutes, having bolted the front door, she had cleaned up the vile mess which the bird had left.

With her duster she flicked away the white peckings of plaster. The afternoon with the gloom of salt rain, the buffeting of the spray and the booming sea closed down around the village. It was warm in The Samphire. Rachel was safe. She could feel herself thawing.

Reluctantly, at six o'clock Rachel pulled back the bolts on the front door and lit the lamps in the bar. Outside, the power of the wind had increased. The door rattled. Inevitably, the regular customers came in, each one casting around the room for Harry and the cormorant. When they saw neither, they shrugged, sat down and ordered their drinks. Rachel felt the ice forming again inside her. She detested the drinkers for their assumption that her husband would be back with his bird, that she would be in her place, meek and silent, behind the bar. No one asked about Harry or mentioned the cormorant. But there were frowns and a raising of eyebrows, a few covert glances at the big clock as an hour passed by.

Eventually the silence was too much. Rachel stood quivering behind the bar and stared at the door. Whenever it trembled with a gust of wind, she put out her pink tongue and ran it over her lips. The customers hunched over their drinks and watched the clock; every quarter of an hour it chimed. As it struck eight a glass which Rachel had been polishing distractedly for ten minutes cracked between her hands, so that she gasped at the sight of the sudden welling of blood from her thumb. She flung the splinters down on to the floor and fled from the bar. When she emerged a moment later she was wearing her coat and holding a big torch. The men in The Samphire followed her, pulling their collars up to their throats, fastening the belts of their raincoats.

Across the promenade she went, pattering down the slippery steps of the sea wall with the men behind her. She flashed the light ahead. The sea was high, there were big white-capped waves pounding inshore. Rachel and her customers crunched over the banks of pebbles, away from the lights of the village. To their left were the crumbling cliffs of the bay which worked their way down to the beach, rich with fossils. To their right, as they trudged along, the sea sucked away the shingle. It was hard to tell whether it was rain or only the spray whipped from the wave-tops which soaked the search party. The pebbles became a confusion of big boulders, treacherously slimy with weed and water. Through the darkness the men followed Rachel as she called for her husband and raked the beach in front of her with the beam of the torch. They splashed through the deep rock pools with the wind moaning around them, they cut their hands on the barnacle-covered boulders, they stumbled over clumps of seaweed.

But there was nothing they could do to help Harry when they found him. In the lamplight he was lying face down among the rough stones. There was a heavy bruise on the side of his head, but the movement of the salt pools and the action of the sea grit had cleaned his wound of blood. It was only a big purple bloom on his temple, like some exotic flower past its best. Harry lay outstretched. The cormorant, oblivious of the direct beam of the torch, held open its black wings and went tap-tap-tap on his cast, so that the chalky crumbs flew like confetti. The cruel beak was through the plaster, into the wounded hand. There was the ringing of horn against hidden steel.

TWICE BITTEN

WHEN IAN MIDDLETON told me he was going to kill himself, I was impressed because I believed he was completely serious. Having known him for six months, I was acquainted with his two obsessions in life, and was flattered that he should tell me of his plan for suicide. Somehow, it seemed such a good idea, sensible and straightforward. We discussed it carefully, combining my attention to the practical details with Ian's natural inventiveness. And quite soon everything was ready.

For sixty years, Ian had led a thoroughly ordinary life, his whole career spent in the orderly routines of a rural boarding school. Apart from a clumsy affair with a young matron, he had had practically no contact with the other sex: to him, women were utterly mysterious and hopelessly out of reach. Once hurt by their appalling fecklessness, he had been resigned to observing them from a respectful distance, often wondering why he should never have what so many of his friends and colleagues seemed to take so much for granted. And he was still hurt at the age of sixty by the recurring memory of a kiss and a sneer, that so much could have been given and then taken away by a careless girl.

One thing had supported him during the monotonous years of classrooms and chalk, the mindless prayers, the awful chores of games, exams and reports, and teas with the headmaster's wife: his obsession with the short-eared owls which came to the Pevensey levels brought each winter a spark of interest. Through the long summer terms, the flat fields were dull and life-less. Only the starlings and peewits walked among the cowpats or gathered under the feet of the sheep. The drains which cut across the levels were full of the whis-tle of coots, and sometimes a kingfisher sped through the rushes, hotter and bluer than the summer sky. But Ian looked forward to the first snaps of frost, when the migrant thrushes arrived for the berries on the hedges, when there were golden plover shimmering among the clods of soil, and, most of all, when the short-eared owls would waft over the reed beds. It was the cat-like faces of the owls which thrilled Ian Middleton and drew him gently through each ordinary year.

But I first met him in extraordinary circumstances, far from his beloved Sussex countryside. He was sitting under a tree on the mud banks of the river Nile in the northern province of Sudan. At the age of sixty, he had broken out and taken a post as a volunteer English teacher. Shortly after his arrival in Khartoum, he had been sent north across the hostile desert to Ed Debba, a little town on the river, to teach in the girls' school. When I was introduced to him, he was drinking beer from a bottle and smoking one of the wretched Suda-nese cigarettes. He was thick-set, with plenty of grey hair, dark eyebrows, and the melancholy expression of a basset hound. Being the only two white men in the town (and indeed within a radius of some hundred miles), we had a great deal to talk about. I had already been in Ed Debba for a year, as a doctor at the little hospital, and I was pleased that Ian had arrived. For the following six months, we spent the balmy evenings by the Nile, with our beer and dates and cigarettes. Ian taught me about the stars: every night they were wonderfully clear overhead and threw their reflections down into the inky water. He told me about his boarding school years, the wounds he had received so long ago at the hands of his one and only love, and he told me about the short-eared owls.

However, some devil saw fit to take Ian Middleton's new life and break it all into pieces. Just when it seemed likely that he would complete that unusual year in the remote but friendly town of Ed Debba before returning to Sussex for an uneventful retirement, a devil chose to spoil all that and waken in Ian something that should have been laid to rest so many years ago. Under the riverside trees one evening, I sat without speaking, content to watch the stars and the water. I saw that Ian was crying. At first he wept silently. His shoulders heaved. I could see in the moonlight the tears come tumbling onto his cheeks and down into the corners of his mouth. Then he was seized by a series of sobs, each one of which tore a sort of rasping cough from his chest.

I said nothing, neither did I touch him. And when he had regained control of his breathing, he simply told me that he was in love with one of the girls he was teaching and could never leave Ed Debba unless she went with him.

Of course, nothing of the kind could ever happen. The girl was sixteen, Ian was sixty. She had lived her life in a tiny village on the Nile, where, since she was five, she had drawn water from the river and made bread in a smoke-blackened kitchen; she had been crudely circumcised on her ninth birthday, and become engaged to her cousin on her tenth. But Ian loved her. I reasoned with him, tried to explain, but he just stood up from the dry mud and hurled his beer bottle out into the Nile. There was a splash. The stars were shattered for a second. Ian stalked away along the river bank.

Worse was to come. There was so much unpleasantness that only a brief account is necessary here. Ian was tortured by his love. He went to the girl's village and made a disastrous attempt to talk to her father. There was the language barrier, of course, but far more insuperable were the barriers of age and culture and religion and understanding. An appalling scene ensued, which resulted in Ian's being punched and shoved from the house by the girl's brothers. Even before he had trudged back into Ed Debba, the headmaster of the school and the police had been notified. Ian spent a miserable week confined to his house (such was the scandal that he would have been assaulted if he had come out), before he could be taken by lorry across the desert to Khartoum, and thence returned to England. That was how the devil dealt with Ian Middleton.

Something of the people's revulsion was then directed at me, as Ian's friend and close companion. I knew that my position at the hospital was not threatened, but it seemed a good time for me to take some leave that was due.

I travelled to the capital and flew to England to be at home for Christmas.

Ian's two obsessions: yes, his beloved short-eared owls and the ignorant young beauty he had been forced to leave behind in Sudan. I telephoned Ian, and we met in Pevensey. And that was when he told me he would kill himself.

We sat together in a little pub, warming our drinks

before a log fire. So different to our evenings in the northern deserts of Sudan. Ian had given up crying. It was as though the ancient wounds had been reopened and then begun to heal again with a film of new and tender skin. Together we organised his suicide. He would fly again to Sudan, where he could travel from Khartoum directly to Dongola, the northern provincial capital. From there, he would take the Nile steamer upstream to Ed Debba. With luck and care, he might arrive unexpectedly, go straight to the school and see the girl for the last time. To be sure, he would be walking into a horrible reception, but he could swallow the lethal dose (which I would have supplied to him) before any assaults or retribution were made. Thus, he would see his darling girl, and quickly die in Sudan. We had covered every detail of travel, documents and currency. Everything was ready.

One piece of business remained outstanding, however. Ian insisted on showing me the short-eared owls. So the next day, after another fireside drink in Pevensey, we drove slowly along the narrow lanes of the levels. It was Christmas time. There was the weak sunshine which gave no warmth, only it raised a little steam from the backs of the wet cattle. The road was muddy and treacherous even at the walking pace at which we negotiated the bends. The light began to fade. As I turned on my headlamps, a few big flakes of snow fell and stuck on the windscreen. Darkness wrapped itself quickly around us and our lights showed up the moth-like snowflakes which tumbled giddily down onto the road and the surrounding fields. The likelihood of seeing the owls decreased with the vanishing light and the deterioration in visibility. I glanced across at Ian. His chin had drooped onto his chest, he was staring down at his hands, folded together limply in his lap. He looked hopeless. I hated the stupid curse which had brought this to him so cruelly, so late. His sixty fruitless years were piling up around him with an increasing, creaking pressure just as the snow was sticking more firmly around the windscreen of the car. There would be no owl. There was simply this slow and random burrowing through the darkness and the bitter cold. It was time to turn around.

I swung backwards into the entrance to a field. The reversing lights glowed against an old wooden gate. There was mud and a thin layer of new snow. Suddenly, the rear wheels lurched and spun. My efforts to move out forwards only sent them spinning faster. The snow fell. Around the car was darkness and the empty fields of the Pevensey levels. Again I tried to coax the car out. It was no good. The more the wheels spun, the more our headlamps jutted upwards into the swirling snowflakes. We were stuck.

Together, Ian and I got out of the car and tried to push it forwards from the mud. Our feet sank into cold water, our hands became numb on the icy metal of the car's boot. We heaved and grunted, swore and slithered. The car refused to budge. Meanwhile, the snow settled. Lit up in the rear lights the fumes from the exhaust rose and vanished into the freezing air. Two clear beams went up from the headlamps and disappeared like long and ghostly tunnels. Ian and I sat in the car to warm our hands. Neither of us spoke. We both felt too cold and too foolish to say anything.

Then Ian said he would try again to push the car, while I stayed inside to coax the wheels free by revving gently. He slammed the door. In the mirror, I could see his face as he leant heavily against the boot. He was lit up by the glow of the tail-lights, so his lined and chiselled features were red and black under dark eyebrows and thick grey hair. He pushed. I engaged gear and eased forward. More smoke rose from the exhaust. In the curling fumes and the orange light, Ian's face contorted with the effort of shoving. The car began to move. The wheels grinned and spun, the headlights shifted higher into the sky. I could hear Ian bellowing with rage and frustration. When at last he could give no more, he began to beat his fists on the car boot. There was a frantic churning of mud before the car slipped backwards into the quagmire of the gateway, embedded more deeply than ever.

I sprang out. But Ian was desolate. He hammered again and again on the car. The exhaust smoke rose around him, the red lights picked out the tears which tumbled down into the corners of his mouth. Then he slumped onto his knees in the mud, with his grizzled head on the cold car boot. His shoulders heaved with sobbing, just as they had heaved on the banks of the star-embroidered Nile.

There was nothing I could do. I waited. Still I had confidence in him, that he could pick himself up, travel to Sudan and make his gesture of contempt in the face of the devil which had broken him.

And suddenly there was a buffeting of wings through the snowflakes. The cat-like face of the short-eared owl loomed fiercely in the headlamps. For a few moments, it hung there like a giant moth mesmerised by the flame of a candle. Ian Middleton wiped the smears of mud and tears from his face and stared up into the darkness.

He drummed again on the car, but quietly this time. He frowned at first, and then he smiled. He could tell that I had seen what he had wanted me to see.

And with this, the owl was gone, swallowed up into the night and the tumbling snowflakes.

LINGERING

Eᴠᴇʀ sɪɴᴄᴇ Rᴏʙᴇʀᴛ Gᴏᴜʟᴅ came to the woodland, there was an uneasy, uncomfortable atmosphere among the ancient trees. He occupied an old caravan which nestled in the dampest part of the wood, which seemed to sprout like a fungus from the moisture of the soil and the rotting leaves and the decaying beech mast. During the daytime, he was seldom in the caravan, and even into the dark evenings there was no light showing at his window. At night, he lit his paraffin lamp when he came in from his persistent, relentless walks through the surrounding trees. Sometimes, then, a curious visitor might see the figure of Robert Gould pacing about inside his caravan.

In all seasons and in all weathers, he walked through the woodland, wearing his orange and black pullover. He wore it every day, whether he walked through the drowsy, fly-infested woodland of summer, the groaning trees of autumn, or the brittle blackness of winter. When the trees were in their full foliage and the floor of the woodland was fresh and shining in green, or covered with the dusty haze of bluebells, then he went quietly about, the orange pullover enabling him to drift inconspicuously among the undergrowth. He merged with his surroundings as a tiger remains invisible in the jungle, appearing then disappearing with disconcerting ease. Even in winter, when the trunks of the trees

51

were black with rain and underfoot the matted leaves glistened, he moved through the woods without calling attention to himself. He was a part of the landscape, he and his pullover, and his caravan which was streaked with the trickling damp and spotted with imprints of dead leaves.

Robert Gould was always in the wood, somewhere. Schoolboys who played among the trees knew he was there, and so did the farm labourers who sometimes cycled along the woodland tracks. Young couples who wandered awkwardly towards the lush expanses of bracken knew he was in the wood, and so did the tidy parents who picnicked with their children. Yet he was seldom seen, only sometimes at a distance, breaking quietly from the cover of a stand of holly or moving across the path, appearing and disappearing. A few times, he had really frightened visitors to the wood. He might suddenly emerge from the bracken, to stand waist deep in its swaying fronds, and wade noisily through it with the same rhythmic efforts of a man who struggles through the crashing rollers of a Cornish beach. Once he had splashed out from under a low, stone bridge, knee deep in the clear water, to terrify a child who was collecting acorns on the path above. The orange pullover camouflaged him discreetly enough for a passing rambler to stumble onto him as he lay outstretched on the ground, peering with fierce concentration into the depths of a tiny pool. Again, a family picnicking among the grotesquely twisted beech trees were suddenly showered with flakes of the grey bark as he leapt and scrambled from the branches, down onto the ground in front of them. The uneasiness was inflicted on the wood by the inescapable, persistent presence of Robert Gould.

But now he is dead. He died among the flames of his caravan on a winter's night. Their glow rose so quickly, so fiercely that it attracted the occupants of the nearest cottages, on the edges of the woodland. The men ran towards the brightness, buttoning their jackets as they ran. Their women followed them, running awkwardly, holding their scarves to their heads. But the flames from the caravan were so hot that the onlookers, who had come only partly to witness the spectacle and really to save the man from the fire, were forced to keep their distance. Against the blackened winter trees, the tongues of flame rose and licked and scarred the icy air. Robert Gould was seen among the blistering roots of the fire, moving with the same intensity and concentration as he had done on many long nights before. The fire took him and he was destroyed in the blaze which, for a small part of that winter's night, illuminated the faces of the onlookers and the contorted boughs of the ancient trees.

But the presence of Robert Gould remains in the woodland, long after the blackened area of burnt ground and the few charred spars of his caravan had disappeared. There is the explosive blundering of pigeons from overhead branches, accompanied by the fine rain of twigs and specks of bark. The deer plunge into the bracken or drift through the half-light of dusk. A fox moves from the side of a stream, appears and disappears, as quick and as lissom as a single, orange flame.

THE BOYS WHO WOULDN'T
WAKE UP

I AN SAT ON HIS BED and looked out of the dormitory
window, down to the drive in front of the school. One
by one, all the other boys were collected by their parents
or picked up in taxis and taken off to Salisbury station.
A succession of cars swept up to the door, crunching
on the gravel, and parked beneath the branches of the
cedar; and then there were kisses and cries of joy as
mothers and fathers greeted their sons. Leather-bound
trunks were loaded into the boots of the cars or the
waiting taxis. He saw Mr Hoddesdon down there, the
headmaster, shaking hands with the parents, ticking a
name on his list as each boy left. Ian sat on his bed and
watched. He was not going home. Soon there would be
no one in the school except him and Mr Hoddesdon.

Ian Stott was seven years old. He was small and neat,
like a vole, with glossy brown hair and wide, brown
eyes. Although he was trying very hard not to cry, his
cheeks shone with tears of unhappiness and fear. He
wanted to be brave like his father, an army officer thou-
sands of miles away in the Falkland Islands. But, when
he thought of his mother, who had written to tell him
she was skiing in Austria so he would have to stay in
school over Christmas, the tears tingled and his heart
seemed to rise into his throat.

Christmas . . . Ian shuddered at the awfulness of it.

He looked around the bare, cold, empty dormitory, at the eleven other beds all neatly made. He sniffed and shivered and he watched out of the window as the last of the cars drove away. He listened as the school fell silent.

It was four o'clock on a December afternoon. Dusk became a misty, whispering twilight. Not a sound, except the wind in the cedar tree . . . Ian Stott was alone in Foxwood Manor with Mr Hoddesdon, the headmaster.

Foxwood Manor was in the Cranbourne Chase, an area of forest and downland in the triangle formed by Salisbury, Shaftesbury and Blandford Forum. A fine house with a single, high, square tower on the east wing, it stood in hundreds of acres of ancient oakwood and beechwood and bristling, black fir plantation. But the school was dwindling to the brink of closure. Years ago, it had had a reputation for academic excellence; but the numbers had shrunk and shrunk, so that Ian was one of only fifty pupils, supervised by five unqualified, uninspired teachers. There was a matron, a cook and a weary groundsman. The buildings were in cobwebby disrepair. The grass was long and untidy on the football pitches; the cobbled stable yard was a carpet of moss; jackdaws squabbled in the great, twiggy nests they had built in the crumbling chimneys. And the house itself was dark and dusty: the corridors and the oak-panelled halls were hung with yellowing photographs and gloomy paintings of long-dead headmasters.

Mr Hoddesdon was the headmaster. At last, when all the boys were ticked off and gone, he limped inside, shut and locked the front door and climbed stiffly up the spiral staircase to his room in the top of the tower. He stoked the smouldering fire, for he was aching and chilled from standing in the freezing dusk. He rumpled the heavy old head of Brutus, the black labrador, and he stared from his windows at the frosty twilight, at the dark, deep woods which stretched as far as the horizon.

Christmas . . . Mr Hoddesdon snarled at the dread of it. Probably his last Christmas at Foxwood Manor, if the school was bound to close. He sat and stared at the fire and thought of the years gone by.

He had spent his life at Foxwood Manor; first of all as a boy evacuated to the country during the blitz, staying on to take Winchester scholarship; later, with a double first from Oxford which could have made him a brilliant young don or at least a master at Eton, he chose to return to Foxwood, to teach Latin and Greek to the brightest boys; and eventually, to become the headmaster, presiding over the school's dismal decline.

Alone . . . always had been. Never married . . . never would be. He never smiled . . . probably he could not. He was seventy, a gaunt and solitary figure who stalked the classrooms and dormitories like a grizzled, grey wolf – hobbling with a stick and growling at the pain in his hips. Brutus was his only companion. For years, for decades, for a lifetime, he had lived in the high tower. Now, he stared into the fire, prodding it irritably until a reluctant, trembling flame stood up.

Another Christmas . . . of waiting and hoping and inevitable disappointment. His last, probably. He glared around the books and photographs which lined his room, at the dust and cobwebs and useless clutter.

As evening became night, he suddenly remembered the boy, Stott, who was still in school. Cursing, he limped downstairs from his tower to the kitchen, rummaged for some milk and biscuits in the pantry and put them on a tray. The place was silent, deserted; only a few optimistic mice skittered in the skirting. Leaving the ground-floor in darkness, he stomped up the stairs and along the corridor to the boy's dormitory.

The little boy was sitting on his bed, staring from the window, although the world outside was black and still. He jumped when he heard the door open, when he saw the man come into the room.

'Stott,' the headmaster said.

'Yes, sir,' the boy said.

'Supper,' the headmaster said.

'Thank you, sir,' the boy said.

Shivering, Ian tried to eat and drink, but the biscuits and milk were a cold, thick paste in his throat. The man stood silently in the middle of the room and looked up and down the row of eleven empty beds. The walls were yellowed and bare and the floorboards were pocked with worm.

'Grim,' the headmaster said at last. 'Hardly changed since I was a boy at Foxwood, sixty years ago. This is my old dormitory, you know. That's my old bed you've got, right next to the window.'

The man snarled with regret and disappointment.

'Hurry up and eat your supper, boy, now that I've gone all the way down to the kitchen and back upstairs again to get it for you. If you're not going to eat it, get ready for bed.'

Then, seeing that Ian was shaking with cold and unhappiness, he added as gently as his growling voice could manage, 'We'll have to make the best of it this Christmas, the two of us. Perhaps we'll go out tomorrow, if the weather allows, walking with Brutus or out in the car. Come along now, stir yourself ...'

While the old man waited, the boy changed into his red and white striped pyjamas, splashed his face and brushed his teeth at the wash basin and then climbed into bed. The headmaster moved to the door. But, as he lifted his hand to turn off the light, there was a rasping at the dormitory window as though someone outside were scratching his fingernails on the pane, and the man whirled round, suddenly startled. He stomped across the room again, stood at Ian's bedside and stared from the window, but all he could see was a glassy blackness.

'What the devil's that?' he exclaimed.

Ian said nothing, huddled in bed with the blankets to his chin, although he knew what had made the noise. It was a noise he was used to, every night in the big, bare room, but he was too frightened to say anything as the headmaster struggled to throw open the window and then leaned over the sill. Freezing air rushed into the freezing dormitory.

'By Jove,' the man said, muttering to himself as though the boy were not there. 'This old thing has grown a bit. I can reach it quite easily now. Here, let me just . . .'

And he stepped back into the room with a fistful of bristly needles from the cedar tree which stood on the lawn below, whose branches reached to the first floor and scratched the glass as they moved in the wind. He held the needles to his face, twitched his nostrils and inhaled the resinous scent.

'That smell,' he said to himself. 'After all these years, it still reminds me.'

Mumbling, growling, snuffling his face in the needles he rubbed in his fingers, he limped to the door again, flicked off the light and went stumping along the corridor . . . too distracted to say goodnight or to close the window he'd left wide open.

Ian waited until the footsteps had faded, until the house was in silence. Then he got out of bed to shut the window. For a moment he leaned out, as the headmaster had done, and he stroked the nearest branch of the cedar. The world was black and empty: no light in any direction, only the deep, dark forest for miles and miles around. Aching with cold, he tugged the window down and jumped back into bed.

There he lay, as the house creaked and whispered, as the needles scratched at the glass. Very lonely, very sad, Ian sobbed until he thought his chest might burst with sobbing, and at last he fell asleep.

*

But the following day was less horrid than he'd thought it might be.

Mr Hoddesdon woke him and hurried him downstairs, where they sat together and ate the breakfast that the headmaster had cooked. The long refectory tables were empty and bare; the panelled hall was gloomy and chill. Mr Hoddesdon was gruff. Brutus sat beside him, lolling a huge, pink tongue, and was eventually rewarded with bacon rind and crusts of buttered toast.

'Coat!' the man said. 'Football socks inside your boots! Gloves! Hurry up and get ready, Stott – five minutes and we're off walking!'

They stepped into crisp, cold, glorious sunshine: Ian in gloves and scarf and Wellington boots; the headmaster with stick and pipe and binoculars and a curious little rucksack slung on his back; Brutus shambling beside him.

At the overgrown ha-ha, Mr Hoddesdon told Ian to leap down into the dilapidated bandstand and find owl-pellets in the dead nettles and the skeletons of willowherb; while the owl itself, blinking and bobbing like a demonic gnome, stared from the rafters at the man and the boy and the big, black dog. The headmaster broke the pellets in the palm of his hand and showed Ian the bones of mouse and shrew and the gleaming remains of beetles that the owl had eaten.

They walked slowly into the woodland. They saw a sparrow hawk, dashing between the trees with a thrush in its claws. They heard jays, shrieking like banshees. They saw deer and hare. The man smelled fox, and the boy sniffed it too, sharp and rank on the cold, dry leaves.

They pushed deep into the undergrowth, to the mounded earthworks of a Roman camp buried in brambles and bracken; and there, where the sunlight was warm, Mr Hoddesdon sat down and opened the mysterious rucksack: a picnic of pies and cakes and ginger beer – a pie for Brutus as well. Later, while the man smoked his pipe, Ian and the dog went burrowing in tunnels of thorn, exploring the ancient, long-lost site.

They walked back in the afternoon. The day grew quickly cold and dark. A grey mist drifted in the woods like smoke. Dusk fell. The forest was silent. Alarmed by the footfalls of man and boy, startled by the scent of dog, deer fled through the plantation and rabbits flashed their scuts. An owl hooted in the freezing twilight. As they broke from the trees, the headmaster and the boy saw the house in the distance, square and black like a huge gravestone.

'Chin up, Stott,' the old man said, seeing how despondent the boy had become. 'We've had a good day out, haven't we? We'll soon get warmed up when we get in. Ever been to the tower? Of course you haven't. No one has, except me and Brutus. Well, we're on our own this Christmas, the two of us. Got to make the best of things. Come on, before we catch our death.'

They crunched across the lawn in front of the house, under the looming cedar, and Mr Hoddesdon unlocked the front door. The hall was dark and very cold. They climbed up to the tower, the man and the dog both limping on the spiral stairs, the boy following, to the secret, private place at the top where the headmaster had lived for so long.

It was a tall, square room, cobwebby and cluttered and chill, with leaded windows on all four sides; a desk strewn with papers and books and photographs, a rumpled bed, threadbare furniture arranged by a little fireplace. While the boy stood and stared, sniffing the smell of tobacco and old man's clothes, Mr Hoddesdon knelt and lit the fire which was already laid in the grate. Soon, the windows gleamed with flamelight. The room was warmer. The man sat in his armchair and the boy sat on the rug, with hot toast and mugs of tea, with carols on the radio . . . scented wood-smoke, the headmaster's pipe, the smell of dead leaves and bracken on a weary old dog . . .

Ian and Mr Hoddesdon were weary too. They nodded asleep in front of the fire. Much later that evening, waking suddenly to find that the fire had gone out, the man shook the boy and led him down the stairs, along the corridor to the dormitory at the other end of the house and put him to bed. Ian fell asleep again, straightaway.

*

He thought he had a dream.

He dreamed that he sat up in bed and saw Mr Hoddesdon in the moonlit dormitory. The headmaster was pacing from bed to bed, stopping at each one to shake at the pillow, tug at the sheets and rattle the bedstead. His face was contorted with panic and terror. He opened and closed his mouth as though he were shouting, but no sound came out. The only bed the man did not shake was Ian's. Again and again the headmaster shook the beds with terrible violence, although there was nobody in them. His face was more and more twisted, blanched by the moonlight, snarling with fear and despair. His throat bulged with silent screams. Until, with a shrug of utter hopelessness, he came to the window by Ian's bed, struggled and struggled to throw it open and then leaned so far out that Ian thought he must surely fall to the ground below . . . only to pause, the panic on his face turning to surprise and bewilderment, to pluck a fistful of needles from the cedar and step back into the dormitory. Then, rubbing the needles between the palms of his hands, sniffing and sniffing them like a wolf, he walked slowly out of the room.

That was Ian's dream.

In the morning, the dormitory was very cold because the window was wide open. The other eleven beds were dreadfully rumpled. Puzzled by his dream, afraid that Mr Hoddesdon would be cross if he saw the untidiness, Ian made his own bed and all the others and went downstairs.

The headmaster looked tired and drawn, as though he had hardly slept at all. He had not shaved, so that his face

was prickly with grey stubble. He grunted at the boy
and then said nothing as they sat in the silent dining-hall
and chewed their toast. At last, pushing back his chair
and standing stiffly upright, he said, 'Wrap up warm,
Stott, and wait for me in the stable yard. We're going
out in the car,' before he shuffled upstairs. Brutus followed him. Ian took the dishes into the kitchen, washed
them and put them away, and then he went through
the corridors to the changing room, where all the rows
and rows of hooks were empty except for his hook. He
remembered the place in term-time, noisy and steamy,
smelling of muddy boys and wet football boots; now it
was bare and silent, swabbed with disinfectant. He put
on his coat and scarf and gloves and went into the yard.

The headmaster was backing his car out of the stable.
It was big and green and very old-looking. It rumbled
and smoked tremendously. It had no roof. Brutus was
sitting in the back, grinning.

'Alvis!' the headmaster barked to him. 'It's an Alvis!
They don't make them anymore! I've had it for years,
since I was your father's age, I suppose! Get in now.
Hurry up!'

The boy slid onto the smooth red leather of the front
seat, and the man eased the car down the gravel drive.
They wound through the woods; they rumbled through
Sixpenny Handley and Tollard Royal; they sped across
the high, bare downs towards Shaftesbury. The town
was lit for Christmas. The headmaster stopped the car
beside a tinselled tree.

'Take the dog now, Stott,' the headmaster said. 'Go
on, Brutus, take the boy for a walk! I've got things to do
in town. Go on, off you go, the two of you.'

For the rest of the morning, long into the afternoon,

Ian and the dog dragged one another about the cobbled lanes of Shaftesbury. They shared a pork pie in a leafless park. As the day grew misty and cold, the boy managed to haul the dog back to the headmaster's car in time to see Mr Hoddesdon and a shop assistant from a nearby store manhandling a wicker hamper into the boot of the Alvis.

'Had a good walk? You've eaten? Good, back to Foxwood now,' the headmaster said. 'Come on, Brutus, jump in! And you, Stott! Collars up, scarves and gloves on. We're off!'

It was a freezing dusk. The sky turned grey. The air crackled with frost. The car ran hot and loud up Zig-Zag Hill and left the town behind. They stopped at the top and let Brutus run for rabbits on the downs; there was a twinkling, twilit view of all England spread below them. The drive back, as darkness fell, was colder still, although the car smelled sweetly of warm leather and burning oil. In starlight, in moonlight, deer drifted like ghosts in the silvery fields. A badger shuffled across the narrow lane. Caught for a second in the headlamps, the fox was a quick, hot flame. The woods closed on either side, bristling and black, and at last there was the school, quite dead and silent and empty. Mr Hoddesdon stopped the car at the front door.

With difficulty, they lifted the hamper out of the boot and put it down inside the panelled dining-hall. Then, they went up the stairs to the old man's tower. This time, as Mr Hoddesdon seemed grey and worn and tired, Ian lit the fire and made tea for him. The dog collapsed on the rug. As the room grew warmer, the headmaster nodded in his armchair. His eyes closed, his chin dropped, his mouth fell open. He started to snore.

Ian waited until the man was soundly asleep. Then, holding his breath, afraid that the headmaster might wake up, he tiptoed around the room, turning over the cluttered knick-knacks, riffling the pages of dusty books, scanning the yellowed photographs until at last he found the one he was looking for. He picked it up from the sideboard and studied the faces: a seven-year-old Mr Hoddesdon and the rest of his dormitory ... a dozen tousled boys, some smiling, some serious, and, lean and tall and frowning, unmistakably the headmaster now snoring in front of the fire.

Ian picked up the photograph and turned back to the man, who was still sleeping: head on chest, feet outstretched so that one of his boots was steaming close to the fire, twitching one of his gnarled, brown-spotted hands. On a little table beside the armchair there was a saucer full of needles from the cedar tree. Kneeling with the photo, Ian took some of the needles and, without thinking, he threw them on the fire. The room was straightaway filled with a sharp, strong scent of resin.

At this, the headmaster woke up. He sprang to his feet. Sniffing, staring madly around him as though he were trapped in a nightmare, he lashed at the boy. He snatched the photograph, shouting so angrily that Ian recoiled from him and sat down on the rug with a thump. The dog fled to a corner.

'Damn you, you interfering boy!' the headmaster cried, his voice blurred, his eyes wild. 'Damn you! Why do you have to meddle? They're all gone! They're dead and gone! They wouldn't wake up! There's only me left!'

And he slumped into his armchair again, clutching the photograph to his heaving chest. Sitting on the rug,

Ian stared at him. For a minute, the only sounds were the spit of the fire, the rustle of wind in the woods and the old man's tortured breathing. At last, seeing the hurt and loneliness on the boy's face, the headmaster grunted. He lit his pipe. He kicked at the fire until it flared alive. And then he started to talk, softly and gently, as though to make up for his outburst.

'Dead and gone,' he said. 'All of these boys in the photograph. Except for me. That's why I came back to teach at Foxwood, so many years ago . . . Shall I tell you what happened? Well, this is the story, and it's all true.'

Ian sat close to the fire, on the rug, too startled and afraid to say anything at all, and he listened to the head-master's story.

'It was wartime,' Mr Hoddesdon began, 'so the twelve of us stayed in school at Christmas instead of going home to the towns which might be bombed. Twelve of us boys, your age, with the headmaster and his wife. They tried to make it fun for us, Christmas Eve, with a bit of a turkey dinner in the dining-hall, with some carol singing, with a Christmas tree and candles. Then to bed, in the dormitory you're in. As I said before, I was in the bed you're using. We all fell asleep.'

The man was quiet for a moment, pulling on his pipe. It had gone out again. He applied another match to it and blew a plume of smoke from his mouth and nos-trils.

'Smoke!' he said. 'The dormitory was full of smoke when I woke up. I woke up and sat up and the dorm was full of smoke. The place was on fire. It was a night-mare . . . I still dream about it sometimes. I jumped out of bed and ran around the dorm, shaking and shaking my friends in their beds, tugging at their pillows. But they wouldn't wake up! It's a nightmare I still have, all these years later, haunting me. In a terrible panic, I went from bed to bed and shook it as hard as I could. There were flames too, from the dining-hall beneath the dorm, licking around the floorboards, licking at the door. At last, since it was impossible to rouse the other boys, I went choking and gagging to the window, struggled to get it open and stuck my head outside for some air. There was a bright moon and deep, gleaming snow. The cedar tree was smaller then, of course, and the branches didn't reach the building at all – this was sixty years ago – but I did the only thing I could to save myself. I stood on the window sill, took a huge breath and leapt towards the tree ... just managed to scrabble at the nearest branch. Tearing at the needles, desperate for a grip, I fell through the branches and dropped to the ground. Even then, I shouted and shouted up at the window. No good! I must have been in shock, with fear and with choking and with the sudden icy cold, because they found me wandering in a kind of trance in the snowdrifts on the lawn, with my hands all ripped and flayed, with my feet and face all scratched.'

There was another long pause. Another cloud of smoke blew from the pipe. Mr Hoddesdon leaned suddenly forward and tossed the rest of the cedar needles onto the fire. They hissed into sweet, scented resin.

'That smell!' the old man said, frowning, shaking his grizzled head as though the memory were as cloying and sticky as the resin itself. 'That's the smell. It reminds me vividly of that terrible night and my leap from the dormitory window onto the cedar tree. By the time the fire brigade had come all the way from Shaftesbury, through the snowdrifts in the lanes, all my friends were dead, smothered by the smoke. All of them dead, because I couldn't wake them up. What more could I have done? It wasn't my fault. It wasn't!'

He was distraught. He steadied himself by gulping the air, like a man drowning. Then he went on, his voice shaking.

'The fire started in the Christmas tree in the dining-hall downstairs. I suppose the headmaster and his wife had had a drop to drink after they'd put us boys to bed, fallen asleep, and the candles set the tree alight. We'll never know. However it happened, I was the only boy who survived. To be haunted ever since.'

For a long time he looked at the photograph, thumbing the faces one by one, as though to impress them forever on his memory.

'What more could I have done?' he whispered. 'They wouldn't wake up.'

With a sigh, he handed the photograph to Ian and told him to put it back on the sideboard. Ian did so. When he turned round again, Mr Hoddesdon was staring into the fire.

'Christmas Eve tomorrow . . .' the old man said.

He leaned to the hearth, rubbing his hands together. He bent his face to the flames and sniffed.

'Christmas Eve again, and as usual, I've got everything ready, hoping and hoping and hoping. Perhaps this will be the last Christmas at Foxwood Manor . . .'

Then, suddenly embarrassed, as though he'd said more than he'd meant to say, he got creakily to his feet and ushered the boy to the door.

'In any case,' he muttered, 'at least there'll be the two of us. Come on now, Stott – it's time for bed. I've got a busy day tomorrow.'

Again, as the night before, he took the boy down the stairs and along the corridor to the dormitory. He waited while Ian changed into his red and white striped pyjamas, while the boy washed his face and brushed his teeth and then climbed into bed. The man looked up and down the other eleven empty beds, shaking his head sadly. He said goodnight, turned off the light and went out. His footsteps faded along the corridor and then there was silence.

Ian was alone in the big, old house, surrounded by the dense, dark, frozen woodland . . . alone, except for the headmaster, haunted in his firelit tower.

An owl hooted in the cedar. The branches scratched at the window. Ian fell asleep.

*

The next morning, Christmas Eve, Ian found Mr Hoddesdon as crusty as ever. Perhaps the man regretted that he'd taken the boy to his private tower and told him the story of the fatal fire. He had no time for the boy. His mind was on something else. He gave Ian a quick breakfast in the chilly dining-hall and then packed him off with a few sandwiches and a flask to go walking with Brutus. Ian did as he was told. It was a steely, freezing day; the sky was heavy with snow. Ian and the dog stepped out as far as the Roman camp, they shared the picnic and they explored together; but it was a cold, lonely, desultory day out. Brutus stared in the direction of the house, whimpering pathetically, finally urging the boy back to the school.

The front door was locked. Ian knocked and knocked, frightened to knock too hard but so cold that he rapped until his knuckles were blue. At last Mr Hoddesdon opened up, with a turning of keys and a shooting of bolts. He peered out, blinking and staring as though he could hardly recognise the boy at all. Then, to Ian's amazement, he let the dog in and slammed the door again. The old man's voice rang behind the locked and bolted door.

'Not ready yet! Nowhere near! Go and clean the car, if you want something to do! Go on, boy! Not ready!'

In gathering dusk, in icy twilight, Ian trudged around to the stables. There, quite lost and utterly miserable, he slipped behind the steering wheel of the car and wept for his mother and father. He was seven years old, and this was Christmas: no friends, no family, no home. No cards, no presents. No love. He sobbed until his little heart ached with sobbing.

At last, conjuring the image of his father, he took a deep breath, gathered the shreds of his courage, slid out of the car and busied himself polishing the chrome on the bumpers and the grille. At least it was a bit warmer in the stable; lit by a hanging bulb, it was quite cosy with the smells of polish and leather and oil. Ian worked until the day outside was as dark as night. When at last he went into the yard and shut the stable doors, he was astonished to find that the world was covered in snow. The school buildings and all the fields and trees were covered by deep, soft, moonlit snow. The world was quite altered. Open-mouthed with astonishment, he went crunching to the front door again.

It was locked. The building was in darkness, apart from the single, golden light high up in the tower. Knocking fearfully at the door, afraid that Mr Hoddesdon would be crabby and cross again, Ian peered through the windows into the dining-hall: pitch blackness. At last he heard the headmaster's slow, irregular footsteps and the door creaked open. Without saying anything, he let the boy inside.

It was very dark in the hall. At first, Ian could see nothing at all, although the smell of the man's smoky clothes was strong. He could smell Brutus too. But then, gleaming in the moonlight reflected from the snow outside, there were glasses and cutlery on one of the long refectory tables. It was set for a meal.

'Light the candles, boy,' the headmaster said softly, and Ian felt the man's horny hand pressing a box of matches at him. 'Light the candles on the table. My hands aren't so steady these days.'

So Ian struck a match. He went down the table on one side and up the other side, lighting all the candles; the whole table was set, six places on each side and one at the head – thirteen settings. As the candlelight flickered and then settled into a golden glow, Ian saw that there were cakes and pies, all kinds of jellies and fruit and syrupy drinks.

'The tree as well,' the man said, and Ian made out the bristling shape of a Christmas tree nearby. He lit the candles on it.

'And the fire.'

The huge fireplace was laid, ready with kindling and fir cones, with stacks of firewood on either side. Ian applied a match, and soon there was a crackling blaze. Mr Hoddesdon sat at the head of the table, and Ian sat next to him.

'Well, shall we start?' the headmaster said.

But they did not start. They simply sat, silent and still, and the feast was untouched.

Bemused, shivering although the hall was firelit and candlelit, Ian sat by the old man. He waited for Mr Hoddesdon to do something, but there was only a long, long silence – not a sound except the crackle and hiss of the fire, the snow and wind in the forest. Ian looked up and down the table, at all the empty places. He looked up at the headmaster. The man had taken a yellowy brown photograph from his pocket and put it on his plate; himself and the other tousled seven-year-olds who had shared a dormitory so many years before. The man stared at it. Ian had never seen such a strange and terrible face in his short, young life.

Mr Hoddesdon was crying. A silvery tear ran down his cheek, into the corner of his mouth and down his chin. It dropped with a splash on the photograph.

The headmaster's voice was so hoarse that Ian could hardly hear what he was saying.

'I know I ought to go up and try again!' he was whispering, smearing the faces of the dead schoolboys with a tear-stained thumb. 'I know, I know! But I'm so tired. Every Christmas I go upstairs for them . . . and there they are. But they won't wake up! I shake them and shake them but they won't wake up! It's a horrible dream that's haunted me for years. So I leave them there and come downstairs again, on my own. Every Christmas for fifty years. Such a waste of a splendid feast!'

He tried a laugh, but it was an ugly sound, bitter with tears.

'Ha! No wonder they don't wake up, for a crusty, bad-tempered old fool like me! Why should they?'

He glanced down at Ian, who was staring incredulously to see this man, whom he had feared so much, blubbering like a baby. The headmaster controlled himself with a deep, gulping breath. He wiped his eyes with the backs of his hands. He leaned down to the boy, 'I don't suppose you'd go upstairs for me, would you? They might wake up for you! Please go for me!'

Too dumbfounded to refuse, and yet hardly understanding what the man had asked him to do, Ian stood up and left the hall; when he paused at the top of the stairs, he turned round to see the headmaster getting painfully to his feet, slipping the photograph into his pocket, limping to the front door with Brutus and going outside. The door clicked shut. Dazed, bewildered, Ian walked the long corridor towards his dormitory. It had never seemed so long, so long and cold and dark, like an endless tunnel. He walked and walked, seeing his dormitory door at the far end of the corridor . . . it hardly seemed to come any closer. He seemed to walk the tunnel for days and months and years. Until, at last, he was there. He pushed the door open and trod softly into the room.

It was bathed in moonlight. The air seemed to swirl with mist, an icy vapour which drifted like smoke. In every bed, a boy was asleep, lips and lashes as bright as the snow outside. No, not in every bed . . . his own bed was empty, the blankets and sheets tossed back. Beside it, the window was wide open. Ian crossed slowly to it, glancing from left to right at the faces of the sleeping boys, and he leaned out as far as he could. He could not reach the cedar tree. The nearest branch was a long way from the window sill. An avalanche of snow had fallen from it onto the ground below, as though . . .

Ian turned from the window. Not sure if he was awake or sleepwalking in a swirling, smoke-filled dream, he went from bed to bed and woke the boys, shaking them gently. One by one, without a fuss, they sat up, rubbed their eyes and stared around. Then, without a whisper or the slightest expression of surprise, they got out of their beds in their red and white striped pyjamas and put on their dressing-gowns and slippers . . . as though they had been waiting for Ian to come for them. Without a word, the boys followed Ian out of the dormitory, along the corridor, down the stairs and into the firelit dining-hall.

There was no one at the table. The hall was deserted. Silent, solemn, their eyes glittering and their hair tousled, the boys stared at the feast and the candlelit Christmas tree. One by one, they sat at the table. Only Ian remained standing, holding his breath, listening to the silence. When he heard a knocking and scratching on the front door, like the knock and scratch of the cedar branch on the dormitory window, he went to open it.

A boy was standing on the doorstep. He was lean and tall and frowning, barefoot; his pyjamas were wet. He said nothing to Ian, but he seemed to stare straight through him at the boys who were waiting to start their Christmas feast. A wolfish, wonderful smile lit his face. He flicked his hands and spattered the snow with a little blood from his fingers. He walked past Ian and took his place at the head of the table. He smacked his hands together, beating off the cedar needles which had stuck to the blood on his palms . . . and this was the signal for the feast to begin. The boy beckoned Ian to come and sit beside him.

It was a glorious party. The fire was ablaze, heaped with logs and fir cones, spitting the blue flames of holly. The Christmas tree twinkled. The oak panels were lit by golden flames, leaping with great, dark shadows. The boys shouted and laughed. They ate and drank until all the food and drink was gone and the plates were littered with crumbs and bones. Then, still seated at the table, they sang carols, their sweet boys' voices high and clear. From time to time, Ian caught the eye of the boy sitting beside him at the head of the table; and the boy nodded back, lifting a bloodied hand.

Outside, the snow fell softly, heavily, muffling the world in a thick, white blanket. It drifted on the open downs, weighing on the deep, dark woods. The fox limped through the trees. The deer coughed and shuddered. The hare was huddled in a snowdrift. The owl floated in the moonlight, its cry echoing in stillness.

At last the feast was over. The carols were done. The fire burned low. Together, as though at a given signal, the boys stood up, blew out the candles on the table and the tree and made for the foot of the stairs. All but one ... Dimly lit by the dying embers, the boy at the head of the table did not move as the others stepped silently to the top of the stairs. There they paused. They turned to watch as the remaining boy stood up and crossed the hall to the front door, opened it and trod into the snow – still barefooted, in his pyjamas – leaving the door open behind him.

Ian followed the procession along the corridor. There was no sound of footsteps, except his own. Again, the corridor seemed endless, like a cold, dark tunnel. Again, the dormitory was swirling with a silvery mist, as dense and clinging as smoke ... As the boys climbed into their beds, slipping off their dressing-gowns and stepping out of their slippers, Ian undressed too. He leaned out of the window, to see the world weighed down and smothered with snow. The cedar branch was out of reach. Stretching as far as he could, he tried to grasp it and shake it, but all he could feel was empty darkness.

And below him, standing on the lawn, was the last boy, barefoot, shivering in his pyjamas. He was staring up at the window, waving furiously, shaping his mouth in a terrible shout but making no sound, gesturing for Ian to make the leap himself.

So Ian climbed onto the sill. He was dreaming. The dormitory was dense with choking smoke. He had to get out. The boy below him was urging him to jump, to launch himself across the cold, black space between the window and the bristling branches of the cedar. Ian stood on the sill. His heart was thumping. The night was icy. He stood there and leaned out and he dreamed he was leaping . . . flinging himself at the tree and grasping with his fingers, tearing his face and hands on the tough, sharp needles . . . falling and falling through the branches and landing with a breath-taking thump on the drifted snow.

But then the boy was gone. It was only a dream, after all . . . There was no smoke in the dormitory. All the beds were empty. Ian stepped down from the sill, shut the window and climbed into his bed. He fell asleep at once.

*

In the morning, he woke from the heaviest of all sleeps and sat up, rubbing his eyes. He had dreamed of laughter and singing and firelight. But now the dormitory was silent: the muffled silence of all the snow outside, the sunlight of a bright, cold Christmas morning. The other beds were neatly made-up. He got up, washed and dressed and made his own bed. When he looked around the room, when he looked out of the window, tantalising shreds of his dream came hovering to the edge of his memory . . . but that was all. He could not remember it.

He went along the corridor and downstairs, into the dining-hall.

No. It wasn't a dream he'd had. On one of the refectory tables there were the remains of a splendid feast – all the plates and glasses and crumbs and bones, all the candles blown out. There was a Christmas tree, whose branches were spattered with wax. The grey, cold ashes of a dead fire lay in the grate. Around the chair at the head of the table, the floor was scattered with cedar needles.

Nobody there.

So cold! The front door was open, and a long drift of snow had blown across the hall. Ian went outside. The world was a crisp, dazzling place. He trod through the deep snow which covered the drive and the lawns. Something was moving there, whimpering at the foot of the cedar. It was Brutus. The dog was scrabbling in a great avalanche which must have fallen from the branches of the tree. Ian waded towards it, calling the dog's name, but it did not even lift its head to see the boy come closer. Whimpering, whining, Brutus worked to clear the fall of snow.

Still and frozen, Mr Hoddesdon lay half buried in a deep drift. The dog was licking his face. The man's hands were bloody and raw, prickled with cedar needles, and the tears were frozen on his cheeks. The yellowed photograph lay in the snow beside him.

The headmaster was not moving. He was not breathing. But, at the last, he was smiling a wolfish, wonderful smile.

THE DREAMING PIG

O N HIS FIRST MORNING AT THE FARM, Ted went to
see the pigs. They were snoozing in the straw of
their low-roofed shed. When he clambered up onto
the corrugated iron which formed a makeshift barrier
around the sty, the pigs did little more than open their
eyes, fix him with a beady stare for a few seconds, sigh
and then doze off again. Ted was intrigued by the pigs.
They lay there in the shed, like porpoises stranded on
the beach. Some of them seemed almost buried, their
legs sticking out from the bottom of the rumbling
mound of flesh. The others rested their snouts on top
and fidgeted through their strange dreams.

Ted knew they were dreaming. He could see it in
their pale eyes which flicked open and shut again when
he climbed up onto the barrier. Their eyes expressed no
interest in him. They only bored through him and then
closed, as though they were trapping a twisted image,
holding it fluttering in the back of their piggy brains. He
would just become a part of their dreams, like an actor
walking onto the stage to speak a few unimportant lines
before walking off again.

Ted was particularly interested in the pigs whose
heads and necks were hidden under the bodies of the
others in the shed. He could see they were alive from
the rise and fall of their rounded stomachs, but he wondered how they breathed and slept under the weight.

Taking up a handful of flints from the ground, he started to lob them at the sleeping creatures, hoping to disturb them and so reveal their snouts. One by one they were awakened, grunting irritably and glaring at the boy who was tormenting them. Two or three remained flat out in the straw, with the steam of their sleep rising gently from their bodies. The other pigs formed up at the back of the shed and snuffled around their trough.

Soon, under the rain of stones which Ted was throwing, only one pig remained lying down. Its back was towards the barrier, so Ted still could not see above its shoulders. Picking up a heavy, twisted nail, he aimed it hard at the pig. The nail struck the animal squarely on the rump and bounced off into the corner of the shed. Very slowly and deliberately, the pig raised itself to its feet and turned towards Ted.

He was horrified by what he saw. What should have been the pig's muscular snout was just a twisted mask. Where the eyes should have been, the skin was smooth and tight, stretched across the brow with no suggestion of the swivelling sockets of the other animals. Instead of tough, leathery ears, the creature had nothing more than stubs of gristle protruding from the sides of its head. With its jaws champing, the pig advanced quickly straight towards Ted's barrier and stormed into it, striking its face into the corrugated iron. It turned immediately, hesitated, then lurched towards the back of the shed, where it stopped, knocking itself against the wall. As though not daring to set off again, it stood still there, only waving its disfigured head slowly from side to side in a curious, snake-like way.

Ted could hardly bear to look at the pig, and yet somehow he could not drag his eyes from it. Slowly all the animals settled down again until they had resumed their earlier position, dreaming and steaming in the straw. Ted had carefully watched the deformed pig, so that he knew which one it was even now that it had buried its head among the other bodies. What could the poor creature know or think? It could not see. It was plain that its hearing was poor, although it had twitched with the others when he had first clambered onto the barrier. The pig inhabited a world of tough, jostling bodies, bodies which slammed into it, lay on top of it, rammed it away from the food trough. Its dreams would be different, of smells and tastes and feelings, and of strange memories which were denied those with sight and hearing. Asleep under the other pigs, this pig would have dreams of which its fellows would be envious, magical and mysterious.

From that first day, Ted came back to visit the low shed each morning. He would wake the pigs with stones and each time the sightless pig was the last to rise from the straw, but it had stopped its pathetic charge against the barrier. Instead it just stood alone in the centre of the sty, waving its head from side to side slowly and rhythmically. Leaving the pigs to settle down again, Ted would set off down the lane, poking his stick into the hedgerows, scuffing his shoes into the rutted track.

By carrying on down the path, he came to the ruined cottage which was about a quarter of a mile from the farm. It stood in an acre of land, bounded on two sides by a high wall. Both the wall and the remains of the cottage were of mud, dried mud containing stones and pieces of wood. The wall had held up well, matted with ivy which held it firmly together. But the cottage was crumbling: the only part of it which had survived was the tall chimney which rose from the furthest side of the building. The ivy had climbed up that part of the cottage and embraced it. The other three walls had been moulded by the rain over the years, until they jutted up into the air more like the grotesque mounds made by termites, or like stalagmites in a cavern.

Ted enjoyed playing along the wall, flushing birds from the ivy. Then he would scramble about the cottage, clambering over the ruins which powdered away under his punishing hands and feet. By using the holes made by rats and the sockets where beams had once fitted, he could climb quite near the top of the chimney. But he could feel the brick of the stack move under his grip, so he always slithered down smartly, knowing it was not safe for much longer. He inspected the scorch marks which blackened the old walls and he drew crude figures with chunks of charred wood, trying to conjure up in his mind a picture of the cottage as it had burned. The farmer had told him how the place had been destroyed by fire. The labourer and his wife had escaped, but their young son had died among the flames. The body had never been recovered. Among the ruins, Ted imagined he could feel the ghost of the scorched child which lingered there. He tried to imagine the smell of smoke, the gagging smoke in his throat, the flames at his face. He could feel the presence of burning and the tormented ghost of that burning.

During those summer weeks of Ted's stay at the farm, the weather had been very hot and dry and he had not slept well. Several nights he had awoken, tired and aching. Then, he had looked from his window down into the farmyard, where all was quiet and still. But twice, in the early hours when he had gazed around the moonlit farm, he had seen one animal awake and moving. While all the others were asleep, bedded down in their snug straw, the deformed pig had been standing up and nodding its awful head from side to side. He watched it for more than ten minutes and it continued the rhythmic movement while the clouds swept across the moon. Somehow, it was excluded from the others' dreams and caught up in its own torment.

But that night Ted had been woken up by the crash of thunder. He found himself sitting up in bed, while the last seconds of the rumble faded away. Less than a minute later, the room was lit up by a massive fork of lightning which shuddered across the sky and crawled away over the horizon. Ted jumped from his bed and ran to the window. This time the thunder ripped the night open with a great dry shout. Down in the farmyard, all the animals were awake, waiting for the next flash and explosion. Quickly, Ted slipped into his clothes and hurried out of the house, closing the door carefully behind him.

He went straight across to the pig sty. Pressed anxiously against the back of the shed, all the animals were standing quivering with fear. Each one was trying to pry the others away from the brick wall. Only the deformed pig was away from the wall, jutting its wretched head straight out and up. Although it was oblivious to the whiteness which leapt over the countryside and only dimly aware of the rippling thunder, its whole body was tense with excitement.

Ted clambered onto the corrugated iron barrier and leaned over. The animals nudged away from the wall a little, only to squeeze back again with the next lightning. Suddenly, Ted was pitched forward as the strange pig hurled itself into the barrier with the full force of its face and shoulder. Before he could get up, the pig rushed past him, followed by all the others in the sty. In a great pack of terrified, unstoppable flesh, they stormed across the farmyard, following their sightless leader.

Ted could only watch as they disappeared. He picked himself up and chased after them, horrified that he could have caused them to escape by leaning too far into the sty. The animals had turned off into a field to the left of the lane, and Ted, thankful for this, quickly shut the gate. At least they would be safe there until the next morning. But, out of the corner of his eye, he saw one pig trotting purposefully down the lane. He ran after it, easily catching it up. The blind pig was following the twisting lane, moving steadily down the centre of the track. While the lightning continued to streak across the sky, scrubbing the fields and hedges, the pig trotted on. It trotted on while the thunder coughed its racking cough. As Ted ran after it, he felt the first heavy drops of rain beginning to fall.

Within a few minutes, they had covered the distance from the farmyard to the derelict cottage. While Ted stood dumbfounded, the pig turned right off the lane and squeezed between the bars of the old gate, into the garden. It went left there, along the side of the ivy-covered wall and then stopped. By this time, the rain was falling regularly and heavily, fizzing off the broad ivy leaves and making rivulets down the mud walls of the cottage. A huge flash of lightning lit up the scene, the pig waiting by the wall, Ted watching from the gate, and the chimney of the cottage silhouetted tall and straight.

Then the pig started off again. It walked slowly and

unerringly towards the building and entered it between the crumbling walls. Standing in the centre of the cottage with the rain beating down onto its broad back, it thrust its face towards the sky. The water coursed down the tightly-stretched skin. It began to move its head slowly from side to side and at the same time to let out a low moan. The sound rose in pitch until it resembled more and more the voice of a young child. It was full of fear and then pain as the note bubbled and gagged in the animal's throat. Before Ted could leave his place at the gate, there was an enormous explosion in the sky immediately above the building. The whole night was stopped dead and lit up with a dazzling light. The pig was a statue, tortured, giving itself up to the sky. The bolt of lightning crackled downwards and struck the very top of the chimney stack with a devastating, electric lick of its tongue. The whole structure wilted, steadied itself, and then collapsed into the centre of the ruin, sending up splinters of wood and a billow of dust. The chimney lay down its whole length into the heart of the house, mud and bricks and rubble. The pig was consumed in a second, while the simultaneous belch of thunder wasted itself into the night air.

Ted stood still under the shelter of the ivy-covered wall, not knowing or caring about the rain and the storm. Only the tortured mask of the pig remained in his mind's eye. He could feel the presence of burning and the tormented ghost of that burning.

THE THEATRE MOTH

THE REHEARSALS HAD GONE WELL. Celia's play was to run for three nights, on the coming Thursday, Friday and Saturday. Even the dress rehearsal had passed smoothly, the actors confident with their lines, the stagehands efficient. Celia was pleased. She had something to prove in the village and at home. The success of her play would silence a few tiresome criticisms.

For weeks she had rehearsed her small cast in the bleak village hall. They were keen and conscientious, but there had been times on those bitter November evenings when her authority had been tested. There were tense confrontations, the amateurs lacking the discipline to follow Celia's directions unhesitatingly. It had taken a while to win their trust, but now that the performances were imminent, Celia could look back on her achievement with satisfaction.

She was twenty years old. After one year at university, she had given up her studies, tired of the immaturity of her contemporaries. It was impossible to study literature in the company of prankish first-year students. They irritated her to distraction with their inane self-assurance and affected eccentricities. Even her tutor, a man in his forties, was a ridiculous dandy. So, to the exasperation of her parents, she had come back to the country, where, to keep herself a little occupied, she was giving some extra tuition to a handful of boys at her father's boarding school. Taunted by her parents and teased by the staff, some of whom had known her as a baby, Celia had put her empty days to good use. She wrote her play, moulding the biggest part so that she could play it herself. Then, in the sharp cold of the village hall, she rehearsed it. Those bitter evenings now seemed worthwhile, the actors speaking plumes of frozen breath across the stage.

However, there was one thing which caused her anxiety. It was not that she or another actor would fumble some crucial lines or even miss an entry onto the stage. Nor was she worried about the efficiency of her stagehands; the props were all in order, and the set was reasonably authentic. Celia had managed to dispel her nervousness at performing in front of her parents and the mocking critics on her father's staff. She was determined to impress them all with the production and even to move them with the moods of her play. But Celia, so brisk and practical, presently so eager to diminish the sense of disappointment which she had recently created . . . Celia was terrified of the theatre moth.

In actual fact, her fear of moths in general was rather self-indulgent. She was disgusted by the creatures, yet on her bookshelves were several volumes devoted to the study of them. So she was aware that the moth in the theatre was a Humming Bird Hawk. Firstly, she knew that it was extremely unlikely that any other moth of its size could possibly survive into the frosty months of the English winter. Secondly, it was noticeably smaller than many other hawk moths, and yet it flew about the chilly room with the disconcerting energy of the projectile after which it was named. Its wings vibrated so rapidly that they produced a high-pitched hum which was obviously inaudible to the men working in the theatre. Certainly it was lovely, the Humming Bird Hawk, but it inflicted upon Celia a fear which tightened her throat and which threatened to twist her face into a strange, pathetic mask. She had seen it several times during rehearsals, but she had disguised her loathing as it hurtled around her. She did not want to weaken her fragile authority over her cast by showing this weakness. Instead, she took the opportunity to identify the moth instantly and to hold forth upon the species' unique ability to remain active in the winter. She was determined that the forth-coming performances should not be disrupted by the creature, and yet it emerged from hiding whenever the body of the theatre was in darkness, whenever there was on stage some brightness made doubly intense by the surrounding gloom. But Celia cuddled her apprehen-sion. She savoured it with the concentration and lust of a man who rolls a few drops of precious brandy around every surface and crevice of his mouth. She shuddered, her skin prickled. In the theatre, she strained her ears to catch the first hint of humming from the dusty wings of her moth. She feared the lick of its long tongue.

The first night arrived. The audience settled onto their hard chairs. Celia's parents were there. They chat-ted pleasantly with people from the village, accepting premature compliments about their daughter. She was a very talented young lady, they all agreed, only it was a pity that she had not persevered with her studies at the university. Nevertheless, she was a great asset to the community. A play was a rarity in the village hall, and that evening they were attending a world premiere. The audience fell silent and the curtain opened on the brightly-lit area of stage.

The play began well. Celia swept onto the stage and spoke with conviction. She hurled her well-turned words about the theatre. The audience rustled in anticipation of Celia's meeting with her lover. But when the two were closeted in the atmosphere of Celia's sitting room, the audience were suddenly struck by a faltering, an uncertainty in Celia's manner. Instead of paying rapt attention to the persuasive words of her lover, she gave the impression of one straining to pick up some distant sound, impatient to quit her present companion, eager to keep a furtive rendezvous. She started up from her seat, recoiling from the arms of her puzzled partner. And then the audience were aware of an obtrusive, metallic resonance. The moth repeatedly struck the table lamp which was the only source of light in the romantic setting. It rammed again and again with its tough body, retreating swiftly before directing itself once more into the light. And Celia stood away from the table, paralysed by her disgust of the awful missile, fascinated by the power of its attack, enflamed by the weight of its wings which shattered the mildness of the light into a thousand separate explosions. Her lover swept aside the creature, which sped into the audience. He took Celia into his arms, shielding the lamp with his own body, as Celia recovered herself and melted convincingly into the strong embrace.

So the play continued. Celia performed distractedly. For her, the stage still flickered with the beat of the wings of the moth. But throughout the three acts, there was no more sign of the insect. Celia was dissatisfied with her performance, having rehearsed an altogether different character to the one she had portrayed on the opening night. Yet the audience were impressed by her and by the play as a whole; they had been convinced by the anxious distraction of the leading character.

The next morning, Celia consulted the volumes on her bookshelves. There was the horrific Death's Head Hawk Moth – it glared up at her from the book. Indeed, the pages fell open naturally at that plate. Many times she had studied this, the grandest and most threatening of moths. Only once had she encountered a live specimen. As a young girl, she had woken late at night to the scrabbling of wings on her window and the movement of her curtains. She had risen from her bed to investigate, expecting to find a small bird on the sill. But she had found her Death's Head Hawk. Curiously, her initial terror was quickly overcome by fascination. Her hands went out to the moth. She cupped it. At first, it remained still. But suddenly it unleashed a frenzy of fluttering, as well as, to Celia's astonishment, a series of very loud squeaking sounds uttered with the same intensity as those of a trapped rodent. The young girl had fainted onto the carpet. When her parents investigated the thump of her collapsing body, they revived her and comforted her. Celia had crushed the broad wings of the moth between her hands and the crippled insect buzzed around the window with the insane determination of a clockwork toy, uncontrolled, relentless. But, although Celia recalled the incident with a grimace, the recurring presence of the Humming Bird Hawk in the theatre now seemed more sinister. The play was important to her. The moth was so beautiful. Celia closed her book gently. The moth had its own importance in the cold village hall.

On the second night, Celia was aware of the self-satisfied faces of her father's senior staff ranged below her near the front of the stage. There had been a few deliberately audible murmurs from them as she made her first appearance, but, as the play progressed, she could tell with satisfaction that the audience were concentrating on the development of the action. In the first act, her performance opposite her lover in the cosy lamplit sitting-room drew a ripple of appreciation from the front rows. Celia responded to the advances of her admirer and warmed to the part. But when, in the second act, Celia faced her father in a confrontation under the glitter of an impressive chandelier, she addressed him with such a studied distance in her bearing, such a stiffness and frigidity, that even her ardour in the previous act seemed unconvincing in comparison. She paused, and she stammered out the remainder of her speech as though wringing each cruel word from her heart to spit it into her father's face. Then she stopped, to stand motionless under the chandelier with an expression of sheer abhorrence frozen on her face. She looked upwards. The moth was darting among the dangling glass, and with each impact it set up a tinkling which grew louder and louder until all eyes in the theatre were drawn to the brightness which had first attracted the insect. In Celia's ears was the insistent humming of its wings and the increasing volume of sound produced by the glass, like the shattering of sheets of ice as they fall from a roof. Within seconds, seconds which seemed much longer to the audience and to the actors, the light from the chandelier was faded down by a stagehand, and when once again it was raised, the moth had departed, back into hiding. Only the gentle, silent movement of the glass remained as proof of its brief but dramatic presence.

After the performance, Celia accepted the warm

congratulations of her friends from the school. Their appreciation was genuine. The play was a success, entertaining the mass of the audience and satisfying the critical demands of the self-important academics. The short interruption in the second act was forgotten, but Celia returned home preoccupied with the moth and the electric effect its appearance always had on her. Since its entry in the second act, she had once again, she thought, failed to play her role as she had wanted, as she had imagined it while writing the play and while rehearsing it. And yet her reserve in the presence of her lover, which contrasted well with her willingness in the earlier scene, and her beautifully sustained aloofness towards her father in the play, had all proved successful, drawing particular comment from the audience afterwards. In her bedroom, she shuddered over the Humming Bird Hawks which shone from the pages of her books. They were repugnant, yet her moth held her with its friction through the air, its galvanic energy.

The play began the third and final performance in the village hall. Again, Celia's parents were there. They had warmed to her over the days immediately prior to the production and they were eager to show their support. Perhaps they had been too hard on her since she had left the university. The success of the play meant a great deal to her and it was important now to be present on the last night of its short run.

But somehow, that evening, the action seemed wooden. Celia moved around vigorously and issued her lines with a certain crispness which did not, however, convince her audience. The other actors delivered their speeches, made the necessary exits and entrances, and the stagehands carried out their duties. But even in the privacy of Celia's sitting-room, the two lovers could not create an atmosphere of excitement or passion. The warmth of the lamp lit up their faces, but in their words and actions there was a lack of conviction which the audience felt as a numbness. In the second act, Celia braced herself to face her father under the whiteness of the chandelier. She wrung her hands and attempted to make her spirited words crackle with bitterness. But over the stage there was a heaviness, a torpor which precluded any truly dramatic exchanges. It was as though a blanket of fog hung about the players. Their feelings were blunt. The play advanced mechanically into the third act.

The climax of the performance approached. Celia waited alone in the shadows of the stage, anticipating the arrival of her lover. The illicit meeting, the clash of the two main personalities of the day amid the flickering rays of a single light had been intensely dramatic on the two previous nights. The characters were powerful, the script was muscular and the scene ominous. At last the audience sensed excitement and romance. As her lover made his entrance onto the stage, Celia applied a match to the candle and the two embraced in its intermittent radiance . . . . But the moment passed. Celia showed such a reluctance to commit herself to her partner that her apparent apathy was transmitted into the body of the audience. The lovers were joined, yet Celia seemed only partly attentive to her lines. She was waiting, she was listening, she was watching the candle, the dancing rays which trembled in the enveloping darkness. Her impatience, ultimately her disappointment, was expressed in every listless move she made. So the play ended. There had been no disasters, no smothered giggles from the audience. Neither had there been any energy, suspense, spontaneity.

Celia was gracious in her acceptance of the compliments which were forthcoming after the performance. But when the audience had drifted away and the actors had exchanged a few pleasantries before leaving, Celia remained in the theatre. She turned out all the house lights and sat on the stage, near the trembling flame of the single candle. A chill settled over the big room. Celia hunched her shoulders and pulled up the collar of her coat. She was weary, weary most of all of waiting. She would wait no longer. But as she cupped her hands around the light of the candle, as she leant over to blow out the little flame, she was suddenly aware of such a high-pitched humming that she could not at first decide whether it was real or imagined.

She was paralysed within the candle's circle of light. Her fingers fluttered in and out of the flame as the humming grew louder. Her eyelids flickered so that the feeble lick of fire seemed stronger and hotter. Her ears shrieked with the overwhelming voice of the moth.

It was only when the insect sped into the prison of Celia's cupped hands that she started from the horror which paralysed her. The moth battered its wings against Celia's palms. She knitted her fingers, the prison shrank, the moth was held in the flame of the candle. In a quick plume of pungent smoke, the candle was extinguished and the room was swallowed into darkness.

There was silence. Celia breathed deeply and became calm again. She would wait no longer. On her fingers was a fine layer of ash, the ash of the strong wings which had vanished into the flame, vanished into the darkness of the empty theatre.

THE DROWNING OF COLIN HENDERSON

COLIN HENDERSON was swept off the deck of the *Thisbe* on the night of the fourteenth of January 1966. There was a fearful storm which had come on suddenly, and the trawler was working hard to beat her way into the safety of the Menai Strait. Henderson went on deck to secure a shifting crate, when an extraordinarily heavy wave collapsed across the ship. He went overboard in a welter of white and green foam.

Weighted down by his boots and his waterproof jacket, Henderson was kept up on the surface of the sea for only a matter of seconds. He saw the lights of the *Thisbe* for a moment before she wallowed and vanished behind the swell. The sky was black. There was no moon. A torrent of spray whipped from the wave tops beat into his face, and he was hurled upwards on the peak of a huge sea before tumbling into a cavernous trough. Then he went under. One final cry for help was checked and swallowed in water. The weight of his clothes and the might of the storm pressed him downwards and he was engulfed.

It was strangely quiet. Henderson watched his hands working in front of his face. They gestured slowly, the fingers opening and closing. They seemed very white with short clean nails. There was darkness shot through with streams of bubbles. It was green and black and silver, with his hands working. A noise of whistling had begun. His neck was hurting. He was aware of being upright and was grateful for this. His legs were lost in darkness, it was only black below him, there was no marbling of silver. The whistling became a long sustained shriek. The light faded. Still his hands, like someone else's hands, continued to move so slowly. The noise grew. A chaos of bubbles blew into his face and then it was green and still. Two things happened together as Henderson died: the shrieking stopped, for a blissful second there was silence, and a marvellous silver blue bubble as big as a cauliflower sprouted from his mouth. For an instant it was joined there. His chest was clenched with pain. Then the bubble was plucked from his lips. It swam away and disappeared in the green distance. He was a dead man.

It was midnight. The storm raged on the surface and the *Thisbe* crept towards shelter. Henderson moved downwards through the darkness. He spun gracefully with the current so that his arms were raised above his head while his legs were moved in a gentle dance. Sometimes he turned head over heels and continued like this, downwards and eastward. A bubble broke from his mouth. It caught in his yellow jacket for a long time and stayed there like a silver pocket watch. As Henderson turned again, the bubble moved on and was trapped in his hair. The bubble spun upwards and shrunk to nothing. His eyes remained open. They did not stare. They were fixed in a level gaze, one eyebrow lifted and held by the frown on his forehead. Henderson's mouth opened and closed as though he were singing. Then a hand would move to his face and brush away an imaginary cobweb. It was peaceful, after the storm on ship. The silence was broken by the mumbling of deep water.

When dawn broke, Henderson surfaced at the mouth of Kalltraeth Bay. He rose into a grey daylight with his face turned up. The storm had become a heavy driving sea into land. The dead man rolled in the waves. His hair stuck and shivered like the seaweed in a tidal pool. His mouth ran with water. There was salt in his eyebrows and eyelashes. If he could see, there was the level land of Anglesey and to the south-east the mountains rose behind Caernarfon. It became lighter and Henderson bobbed through a gentle sea. His heels in the heavy boots touched land while his stiffening fingers clutched at the movement of weed. There was a cormorant fishing. It beat its way out of the water when the yellow jacket creaked. A cloud of gulls fell into the waves and looked at the man. One bird jabbed its beak once into Henderson's beard and flapped away, screaming. The gulls moved off to the sands of Malltraeth.

All morning he swam slowly in the shallow water. It was warmer and there was a clear sky. He turned over when the swell came, his face pressed into the green clean sea. Into the bay as the tide pushed on. There was rubbery weed before the bottom cleared to a firm hard sand. The tide stopped and waited. The sea held. The man lay on the sand with his face to the sky. When the sea retreated, Henderson remained, like a man asleep. He lay on the sands in his yellow jacket and boots, with his hair drying in salt sunlight. White lips. Seaweed skin. Empty eyes. A throat full of brine. A dead man.

Crabs collected at his finger nails and tested the flesh. It was very soft. They began to feed there. The heron came and was afraid. Curlews fled with a skyful of sad songs. Only a pair of crows stopped to see and soon they saw it was safe to stay. Their heavy beaks broke open the skin on Henderson's cheeks.

But a man came, attracted by the yellow jacket. And soon they carried Henderson from the estuary.

It was the fifteenth of January 1966. A woman arrived to see the dead man. They had cleaned his face and put powder where the crows had been. Henderson had closed his eyes and his mouth. They asked the woman: 'Is this man Colin Henderson, of the *Thisbe*?'

'Yes,' she said, and she touched her husband's lips.

THE LATE MR LEWIS

T HE BEGINNING OF DECEMBER, 1959. No snow, not
yet. A crackling of ice, from Rhos-on-Sea to the
woods of Pwllycrochan.

I was a little boy at boarding school. The Holy Ghost?
The perils and dangers of this night? I remember being
told of such things. But no one explained what they
were or what might happen.

I was seven years old. I remember the chilly dormitories and the frozen playing fields, the clattering din of
the dining room and the hymns we sang every morning
and evening. I felt very small and cold, and sometimes
hungry.

I remember some of the teachers for the things they
didn't tell us, rather than the other way around.

There was Mr Newton, who made us stand by our
beds in the dormitory while he asked God to protect
us from 'the perils and dangers of this night'. Then he
would tell us to get into bed and he turned off the lights.
But he never told us what the perils and dangers might
be. I remember lying in the shivery darkness and wondering, afraid.

And the Reverend Job, who talked about the Holy
Ghost, as though we all knew it and had seen it many
times. But he never told us what it was or what it might
do to us. I still don't know, nearly sixty years later.

Mr Lewis was different. For one thing, he didn't live

in school with us boys, like a lot of the unmarried teachers. And he was older than them, a lean, sinewy man
who cycled from Rhos-on-Sea every morning, along the
Colwyn Bay promenade and puffing up Pwllycrochan
Avenue. I remember looking out of the dorm window
on dark misty mornings, as we got ready to go downstairs for breakfast, and seeing the light of his bicycle
coming closer and closer. I remember how the light
wobbled and swayed from side to side, as he struggled
up the slope and into the school drive, and how he
always rang the little bell on the handlebars, so we knew
he was in time to join us for breakfast. He was proud of
being punctual. Late? Mr Lewis, late? Never.

Mr Lewis taught me things. In the summer term
he took me into the cricket nets and showed me how
to bowl a googly. In the autumn, he showed me the
owl-pellets beneath an old oak tree, crumbling them
onto the palms of my hands. And yes, he whacked me a
few times as well, when he was on dorm duty at night,
for talking after lights-out. I remember the sharp sting
of pain from his cane. That was Mr Lewis. He explained
things. He showed me how to do things. He was strict,
but I understood what he meant.

But then he was gone, suddenly, in the cold winter of
1959. Something to do with the Holy Ghost? Perils and
dangers? Maybe. Let me tell you what happened, what
I saw with my own frightened little eyes, and then you
can decide for yourselves what it meant . . .

It was December, nearly the end of the Christmas
term. We'd been practising for the Carol Service. I
had a sweet voice and I was chosen to sing the opening
verse of Once in Royal David's city, unaccompanied,
as we would proceed into the church. Mr Lewis chose

me. He was a Latin teacher, but he coached the choir as well – and he told us it was a tradition that we held the Carol Service at night, in the church at the bottom of Pwllycrochan Avenue – an important event, with lots of parents and other grown-ups in the congregation.

Over the last few weeks of the term, he rehearsed the choir through all the carols. We worked hard on my solo. As the time for the service approached, I became more and more nervous. But I knew, in my anxious little boy's heart, that Mr Lewis would be there, he would hold my eyes and give me courage and it would be all right.

On the night, we wrapped up in our coats and scarves and we trudged down the hill towards the church. Trudged, yes, we could hear our footsteps ringing, because the frost was so hard, the darkness was so deep and silent. It was Mr Newton who led us choirboys down the avenue. He told us that Mr Lewis had gone home to Rhos-on-Sea for his tea and would, of course, cycle back and meet us at the church in plenty of time.

So cold. So dark. The trees loomed around us, huge black shadows. As we came to the church, a few flakes of snow were falling.

But Mr Lewis wasn't there. Mr Newton was beckoned away from us, where the headmaster and some of the other teachers were huddling in the doorway. Their faces were strangely white and anxious, and they spoke in muffled whispers.

After a moment, the headmaster turned from his colleagues, ushered a few shivering parents into the church, then he gestured at me to lead the procession of choirboys inside. I did so. Somehow, I held my nerve and I sang the first verse, Once in Royal David's city, on my own. My voice was shaking. It echoed coldly in the shadows of the ceiling.

Somehow, we got though the order of service. In the Bleak Midwinter... Hark the herald angels... Silent night. At last it was over. I led the choir out of the church.

The world was changed. The snow was falling heavily, swirling flakes as big as a million moths. Over everything there lay a deep white blanket of snow. Not a footprint. Nobody, no bird or animal had ever touched it.

As we huddled together outside, we could hear from the open doorway that the headmaster was talking, loudly and clearly, to the teachers and parents who were still sitting in their pews.

I strained to hear. He was saying how very sorry and upset he was, how everybody was so sorry and sad and upset. He was talking about Mr Lewis. All of us choir-boys stood in the doorway and we listened.

The headmaster's final words hung in the air, frozen forever in the chill of the church. He said that our Carol Service, our songs and our prayers this Christmas should be dedicated to our dear friend and colleague, Mr Lewis, who would be so sadly missed – the late Mr Lewis.

Late? Mr Lewis, late? I remember how suddenly relieved I was, because I didn't know what it really meant and throughout the service I'd been wondering what had happened to him. So he was late, that was all! Maybe he was coming, he was on his way right now!

And sure enough, in the silence that followed the headmaster's words, I heard a sound I'd heard every morning of my days at the school.

The other choirboys didn't seem to hear it. With white, frightened faces they remained in the doorway of the church.

I broke away from them and ran across the snow towards the road. I stood there, alone.

A light! Yes, there was a light coming up the avenue, wobbling and swaying from side to side.

A bell! Yes, the ringing of a little bell. Closer and closer it came towards me, a bicycle appearing from a swirl of snowflakes. My heart lifted with a sudden happiness.

Until I saw that there was nobody on the bicycle.

No one. The light swayed and wobbled. The bell rang. The bicycle passed so closely to me that I could have reached out and touched it. But there was no one on it.

It went by. I watched it going, up Pwllycrochan Avenue, up towards the school. It disappeared into the darkness. And as I stood there, for what seemed like a minute or five minutes, the track of its tyres disappeared in the snow.

I didn't tell anyone what I'd seen. Never – until now. I didn't know what it meant. And I still don't know, nearly sixty years later.

THE DEVIL BIRD

ONLY LAST SUMMER, David had realised how very special the swifts were. They frightened him, being so special. Their wings were longer than their bodies, so that, folded, they tapered and joined an inch past their tails. In flight, they were perfection. It was clear that they had been designed as true specialists, so that anything could be accomplished in flight. He had seen them courting and mating a hundred feet above the ground, and he knew they could sleep there too, still flying. He had heard them called 'the footless birds', and had checked the name with his books. So weak and tiny were their feet, that they could grip and perch for only a short time, and only high up from the earth, so that, to resume flight, they simply released their grip and spun away while falling. Certainly they were special birds.

A year ago, David had come across a swift stranded on the ground, in a thicket. It was the first time he had come close to one, and looking at it, he remembered: this was one of the screeching devil birds which spun among each other like splinters from a thorn bush, taking insects in their gaping mouths. There was something very dark and sinister about it, a suggestion of caves and cliff sides, of chills and damp. The bird lay in the brambles, with its sickle-shaped wings outstretched. One of them was broken. He looked closely at the cigar-shaped body, the tiny feet and the wide mouth. But chiefly he looked at the wings. A teacher had come by and David called to him, led him to the swift. Together, they had looked, without saying anything, until the teacher had told the boy to wait for him, away from the thicket. But David had turned and watched, had seen the man press the heavy stone onto the bird, pressing it down into the ground. And he had been frightened by the swift, and frightened by how special it must have been for this to happen.

This year, he was waiting for them. As always, the swallows came first. They were beautiful, at ease near people and their homes. When they arrived, they twittered around the windows and the chimneys, so relaxed and close that he could clearly see their colours. These colours told him of their great task, the accomplishment of their annual migration. On the swallows' backs, there flashed the moods of the seas and the skies. At their throats, they bore the blood of others who had failed. And on their bellies, there shone the whiteness of their purification, their annual cleansing. Yes, the swallows were lovely, but David thought he understood them. They liked being liked.

Two weeks later, the swifts came. After the swallows, their darkness and their distance from the house gave him a small chill, watching them and hearing their hard screaming. He wanted to believe the old mysteries about the devil birds. It was true that they disappeared towards the end of the summer and only came back after the spring, but their disappearance could have no connection with that of the swallows. A century ago, it was said that they went to the moon. David could imagine their darkness speckling it, making the shadows on it which he could see when the moon was full.

Yes, the dark patches were hordes of swifts which had left the earth for the winter months. Others had believed that they slept in the mud at the bottom of ponds and streams. This explanation too pleased him. It made their darkness and the chill and the damp seem believable.

He walked along the narrow path which started at the old bridge. The scream of swifts went on continuously overhead. He had seen a dipper whirring downstream, to perch, bobbing like a clockwork toy, on a rock. A pair of buzzards had lumbered from the branches of a tall tree before soaring away effortlessly, with hardly a movement of their broad wings. But the swifts had no connection with the earth. They hurtled around in the blue space, always screaming their independence.

David followed his usual route, his destination the same as on previous days. Among the densest under-growth a hundred yards from the river bank, there was a huge ants' nest. He pushed his way through the brambles, crouching down and holding his arms up around his head. The thorns plucked at his shirt, but he pressed on until he was standing over the seething mound of ants. He liked to take little twigs and dry leaves and place them on the nest, and watch the ants organize them-selves into working parties to shift them. They worked on the sticks like gangs of convicts, watched over by their wardens. Often the ants would go swarming over his shoes and up into his socks, so he would have to stamp his feet or brush them off lightly with his hands.

Suddenly, quite close by, the scream of a swift took his attention from the insects. It was different from the airborne, rasping cries he had heard before. Looking around, he saw a bird flapping helplessly among the brambles, hanging like a bit of old rag, beating itself against the thorns. He quickly fought his way from the ants' nest and stood near the trapped bird. In between the frantic efforts to free itself, it lay over the spikes, heaving with exhaustion, just turning its head and staring. Its beak was open, and David could see the wideness of its gape.

As gently as he could, he picked the bird from the bushes. He carefully folded back the long wings, laying them flat along the side of the body, firmly keeping them in place. He had the swift in his left hand, with its squat head sticking out between his thumb and fingers. With his right hand, he caressed its throat. The bird hissed and hissed. The pounding of its streamlined body grew less and less.

David looked up at the other birds. That one of their kind had come to earth was of no concern to them. He held the bird up as high as he could from the ground and measured with his eyes how much clearance it would have if he was to attempt to return it to its element. But, knowing it was special, the act of giving it back must be special. He would as soon fling a fish into the stream, see it cartwheeling helplessly in mid-air before splashing onto its side into the water. For this creature was not of the earth. It must be returned in a fitting way.

So the boy undid the top two buttons of his shirt with his right hand, then gingerly placed the bird between the cotton and his chest. It did not move, while, with both hands free, he quickly did up the buttons to his throat and made sure his shirt was properly tucked into his trousers. But as soon as he began to walk, the bird began a frenzy of beating and screaming inside his shirt, scrabbling with its feeble feet, lashing with its marvellous wings. He continued walking to the foot of an old pine tree which grew near the side of the river. Still the swift screamed and beat itself against the boy's chest.

But, by the time he had set his hands to the branches and begun to climb, the bird lay still, just pounding its heart and gasping. Sometimes it would hiss. But it had spent its force for a while. David worked his way up slowly, avoiding contact between his chest and the tree, just climbing loosely from branch to branch. He concentrated hard on staring at the rough bark and gripping keenly with both hands. As he went higher, he spent longer checking every hold of hand and foot before taking each step. The trunk became thinner and thinner and the bristles of the tree became shorter. Soon he stopped climbing, at the highest stable part of the tall pine.

He rested with his body wedged among the branches. From there he could see right back to the bridge, and watch the cars and lorries crossing it before climbing up to the moor. Below him, the river ran on, but he could hardly hear its movement. Only he could hear the movement of the trees and feel their swaying.

Letting go with one hand, he undid the top buttons of his shirt. He slid his hands down and quickly took the bird. There was no time to arrange it. He had only to seize it firmly and withdraw it from his shirt. When the bird came out into the light again, David was holding it by its body and one wing. Immediately it cut at him with its other wing, until he could hook his arm securely around the trunk of the tree and concentrate on taking the bird properly in both his hands. Feeling itself pinioned, it just hissed and panted, and the boy waited until it was calm again.

Then he stood up on the branch, holding himself at

arm's length from the trunk. As he had done before, down among the brambles, he raised the bird as high as he could above his head, away from the needles of the pine. He did no more than open his fingers. The swift panted on his palm. It turned sideways so that its long wings fell away from his thumb, gripping with its feet into his skin. It simply held both its wings out open, two wonderful scythe-shaped wings, released the hold of its feet and fell away into the air. As it fell, it tumbled over twice. David watched it fall. Like a fish suddenly replaced in the river, it lay back in its element, dazed, confused. But then it gave an electric clap of its wings, wheeled away to its left and flung itself up into the air, describing one enormous arc and screaming lungfuls of screams into the sky.

David climbed down the tree. When he reached the ground, he found he was shaking. He could not stop himself from trembling. He felt a chill pass through him. He felt the sharp black splinters in his hands.

THE BLACKBIRD'S SONG

A S A MUSICIAN, Heather Cochrane was both thrilled and exasperated by the song of the blackbird outside her sitting room window. The purity of his fluting was something she knew she had never achieved, not even in a professional career that had spanned twenty-five years. The golden notes tumbled from the golden beak, coined from somewhere deep within the blackbird's breast, but then, after every phrase, the song was thrown away in a breathless rattle, just a flurry of random notes such as she would hear from lazier pupils. The blackbird was a profligate genius, generous enough to visit the cherry tree and serenade her every evening, but almost insolent in the squandering of his gifts.

Heather sat near the window and listened to the bird, brittle with the tension of waiting for imperfections, in voices and laughter and song. A lifetime of listening had trained her to a high pitch of awareness and she was wounded by any jarring sounds. She could never escape and relax: even in her dreams, she winced. So the songs of the blackbird were both a delight and a torment to her. Her thin neck and wrists were taut with pleasure at the mellow phrases and she gripped the arm of the chair with the long fingers of her left hand at every careless trill which blotted the beauty of the music.

It was like this each evening, until the blackbird stopped singing and fled into the woods with a chattering cry. With nightfall, Heather unclenched a little, soothed by the notes of the owls and the soft wind in the branches of the cherry tree.

For twenty-five years, Heather had received the unstinting acclaim of public and critics all over the world. New York, Paris, Tokyo, London, Rio de Janeiro, Sydney – in every great city, she had heard the rapturous applause of her audience, had left the stage with her arms full of brilliant bouquets. Her talent had been obvious even as a child and, as she turned into a delicately beautiful woman, her reputation spread, enhanced with each performance.

On stage, surrounded by the bulk and paraphernalia of the orchestra, dwarfed by the conductor, Heather looked small and vulnerable. Audiences held their breath when she appeared. Surely this pretty child, fine as a Dresden doll, could not match her flute against such overwhelming forces? But from the moment the instrument touched her lips the orchestra became her toy. It surged and swelled and softened at the nod of her head. Even the baton seemed dominated by the beat of Heather's foot. And the audience was held by the magic of her breathing, by the tenderness of her fingers . . .

She married in London and her husband, Harry, managed her career, arranged concerts, rehearsals, recordings, interviews, flights and limousines. For twenty-five years they were always together and, apart from the critical acclaim, Heather's success brought them considerable financial reward. They worked hard, loved the tempestuous pace of a busy calendar – and the money enabled them to enjoy a sumptuous lifestyle. At forty-five, her career was planned ahead for years to come, with bookings in concert halls on every continent.

And then the accident happened. Heather knew nothing about it, sleeping through it all. One night, after a great success in Frankfurt, they were driving along the autobahn, glad to be alone together after the exhilaration of the concert, the encores, the roses. Heather slept in the back of the big car, a rug wrapped around her legs and Harry, smiling to see her so contented, eased his foot harder on to the accelerator and let the car swallow mile after mile of the deserted motorway ...

A puncture sent the car ploughing across the central barrier, cartwheeling many times before smashing into the pillars of a flyover. No other vehicle was involved – but Harry was killed and Heather woke up four days later, in a hospital bed, her head swathed in a bandage, her right arm completely numb. In a week, she walked out of the ward, helped by her daughter, Sarah, and was escorted tenderly back to England. Harry was buried. Heather went to their house in Somerset, to recover from the shock of the tragedy, spend her grief, and convalesce.

And then it became apparent that the injury to her arm would never mend. The doctors operated on her wrist and elbow, explored those mysterious channels which had hitherto transmitted the message of Heather's music from her head to her fingers. And achieved nothing. The fingers and thumb of her right hand were utterly dead. Even when a little jewel of blood erupted from the ball of her thumb with the insertion of a needle, there was a complete absence of feeling, of pain.

In Somerset, Heather burned herself a few times in the kitchen, alerted only by the smell of scorched flesh. The doctor would come and treat the burns, to prevent infection, but it seemed so irrelevant to her.

She stayed in the house, very comfortable and afflu-
ent, taught a few promising young flautists, for whom
it was a great honour to sit at the feet of the renowned
Heather Cochrane. As the students played, she beat
time with her right arm, flailing the fingers in front of
her pupils' faces. It was her trademark: she knew they
would go away and tell their friends about the limp
fingers, the scars and scorch marks. But it always hurt
her that she would never play again, never even demon-
strate a simple piece for the benefit of her protegés.

Her flute remained locked away in its case. Soon after
the news broke that her career was ended, she received
a few insensitive telephone calls from dealers wishing to
buy it and, feeling outraged and wounded, she would
slam down the receiver.

Heather's daughter visited often, cycling over from the
nearby village where she lived with her husband. Sarah
was musical, too, a more than competent pianist, but
marriage and children had been her choice, not a career
in music. Sometimes she would come and play for her
mother, or else they would just sit in the sunlit room
and listen to the blackbird. Sarah tried to draw Heather
from the melancholy that engulfed her, but her mother
could not respond. Heather's days were spent walking
along the Somerset lanes, her evenings alone with her
records.

Now it was May. The cherry tree was laden with pink
blossom and, as the sun faded that evening, the tree
remained alight, as though it had absorbed the brilliance
of the day and could radiate it like a candle.

Heather rose from her armchair. She had seen no one
since the milkman's visit that morning. Her walk in the

afternoon had been solitary – and she was lonely. She would never have admitted it, even to Sarah, for there is a peculiar sense of shame attached to loneliness, as all lonely people know. But it was the truth.

She stood at the open window, uncertain. The blackbird was curiously subdued – it had experimented with a few wheezy scales, and fallen silent. Unthinkingly, Heather puckered her lips and tried to whistle – but the air blew out without producing a note. As a little girl, whistling was forbidden – it was considered unladylike – but there the blackbird sat, silent among the blossoms. Again, Heather tried. This time, there was a trace of a note. Again and again, she licked her lips and blew, until suddenly she produced a single, piercing note which sent the blackbird chattering from his perch, to disappear into the dusk of the rhododendrons. And Heather smiled.

In the morning she tried again and amazed herself with the clarity of tone, just a single fluting note, but pure enough this time to make the blackbird halt his song and turn a bright, inquisitive eye on the woman at the window. He froze and listened to the repeated call.

As spring lengthened into summer, the blackbird was in the cherry tree earlier in the mornings and later into the soft, balmy evenings while Heather practised her whistling, enlarging her repertoire of notes.

For Heather, as a musician, it was not enough to fling away a popular tune, in the jarring fashion of her milkman: each new sound she made was polished until it began to have the lucid depth achieved by the bird. Only then, after repeating a note many times, would she allow herself to incorporate it into a scale or an *arpeggio*. There must be a period of intense polishing before the note was used, as though a coin was minted and must be burnished to a high gloss before being accepted as currency. And every morning, she joined the blackbird in the garden for a rigorous session of practice.

Using her tongue, Heather broke a continuous note into trills and quavers, worked on the delicate shades of pitch which the bird had perfected. And in the evening, she wet her lips with a little red wine and worked with the bird until dusk. Then, as always, he vanished into the woodland to join the other birds in a cacophony of songs and trills.

Soon she thought she was ready, after weeks of rehearsal at the open window, to reach for the sheet music and see what could be made of it all. For the first time in more than five years, she took out her flute case and unlocked it. The instrument shone, exposed to the light after a long confinement in its velvet-lined coffin. Heather stroked it lovingly with the fingers of her left hand, felt it hard and cold, devoid of life. Then she laid her useless fingers on the flute – and, as expected, felt nothing at all. Under the instrument she saw some sheet music, so she took it out and went over to the window.

There, in the afternoon sunlight, Heather sat in her armchair with the music spread on her knees. It was one of her favourites, lyrical and strong, Drigo's Serenade from *Les Millions d'Arlequin*. The tune came easily. She ignored some of the trills in order to master a creaminess of tone. The details might come later, after much more practice. Deciding not to persevere just yet until the piece was polished, as she would have done with her flute and as she would have advised her pupils, she turned to another sheet – *Minuet and Badinerie* by Bach. It proved straightforward enough to whistle from sight, deceptively simple. She must not cheat and go too slowly – but speed would come, possibly at the expense of clarity. Her tone suffered less with slower, more haunting melodies, such as she had rehearsed under the tutelage of her blackbird. *Haru no Umi* by Michio Miyagi, which her husband had loved so much, was good first time and would improve.

Heather was pleased. An hour went by and she had run through a dozen pieces which, since the accident, she had only heard a few times on her record player. She felt again the old, satisfying weariness, forgotten since her flute was laid to rest. But that night, she only listened to the blackbird. 'Let the master play,' she thought, 'I will listen and learn more.' And, much later, she slept the sleep of the dreamless.

From then on Heather's days were once more full of music – her music. She knew that her whistling bore only a passing resemblance to the flute, although for sheer quality of tone she felt that the flute was surpassed, as it must always have been surpassed, by the sweet voice of the blackbird. But for speed and range and agility, her whistling was very limited; she would resign herself to polishing a small repertoire and filling her days with music of her own making.

Still she practised. More and more, she listened to the blackbird: not just listening, with the bird a part of the lovely rural scene, but blanking out every other sound of the garden and admitting only the bird's song to her well-trained ear. He had been her inspiration, and still she learned from his whistling. There was something in his tone that she had never achieved with her flute. Now she was closer to its achievement with her own lips, in spite of her paralysed fingers. The purity she heard each evening from the branches of the cherry tree was within her reach. Time, patience and perseverance would tell.

The summer went by and Heather was happy. Sarah noticed with pleasure that her mother had escaped the magnetic pull of melancholy and that once again she had that spark of vitality that had captivated her audiences. Slim and fine, delicate as a porcelain figurine, she exuded the strength associated with youth or love, two qualities she thought she must have lost for ever. But Heather kept the reason for her renewed peace of mind a secret, a secret between herself and the blackbird.

One evening, at the end of August, Sarah arrived unexpectedly. It was warm and she had walked the last mile of the journey, better to enjoy the scents and whispers of the hedgerows. She pushed her bicycle up the drive of her mother's house, stopping for a minute to admire the song of the birds. There was the blackbird, velvet black with a beak of gold, singing for all he was worth in the cherry tree.

Sarah knew that her mother would be sitting by the open window, listening, her head back and her eyes closed. So she leaned the bicycle by the path and walked carefully towards the front door, not wanting the ticking of the pedals and the crunch of the tyres to disturb the song. But when she drew closer, she stopped again at the sound of the flute which came drifting to her from the house.

Yes, it *was* a flute! A flute . . . and yet, somehow different . . . Sarah listened. The music was splendid, with a greater depth of tone than the flute, more penetrating, warmer. It must be a flute, one of mother's more promising pupils perhaps, or a recording. Sarah went quietly to the door and entered, without knocking. But when she closed the door, it clicked and the music stopped at once.

'It's only me!' Sarah called out, and she walked into the living room.

Heather was standing near the window, frail against the fading light. 'Oh, hello, darling,' she greeted her daughter. 'I didn't hear your bicycle. Have you walked all the way?'

Sarah looked around the room. There was no one else there, no record on the turntable.

'Oh, no. I left the bike halfway down the drive,' Sarah explained. 'I didn't want to disturb your blackbird, he was singing so beautifully.'

They both sat down and for a moment, said nothing. The garden, too, was silent, then Sarah spoke. 'What was that music I heard? It sounded like a flute. Was it a record?'

Heather looked away. 'Must have been the blackbird,' she said. 'I haven't listened to any music today.'

'Oh no,' Sarah protested. 'I know the blackbird by now. He carried on singing when I walked by the tree. I thought it was a flute.'

Then she saw, on the piano, her mother's flute case. It was open. There were several sheets of music, books of musical scores. Through the gathering twilight she tried to peer at her mother's face, but Heather would not turn to look at her. The flaccid fingers dangled, useless. No one spoke. Heather and her daughter sat and listened to the silence of the garden. Ten minutes of silence . . .

'Play for me, Sarah,' whispered Heather. She stood and went to the window. 'There's some music open on the piano. Don't say anything, I want you to accompany me again, like you used to. We can still make some music together.'

Shivering, her daughter moved to the piano, sat down and turned on the little lamp. It cast a bright white light on the sheet of music and as Sarah began to play, Heather faced the garden and laid her hands on the window-sill.

The air was heavy with honeysuckle as the first note rang out and there was a momentary hesitation in the hands of the pianist when flutelike notes sounded, but then they played the accompaniment with strength and composure as they had done more than five years before.

The flute was never so rich! From Heather's lips, the notes sprang and grew and blossomed, falling into the warm night air like petals from a cherry tree. The room was full of music that melted into the fragrant garden. The scents of the roses and the honeysuckle and the cut grass breathed in the power and tenderness of Heather's notes as the music rose and fell. And when it had finished, there was a silence such as that garden had never heard before.

Until, from the darkness of the cherry tree, there came another song.

The golden notes tumbled from a golden beak, coined from somewhere deep within the blackbird's breast. And, for once, the music was left unspoiled. The blackbird stopped on a note of perfect purity and then fled into the velvet shadows.

THE PROGRESS OF
JOHN ARTHUR CRABBE

M RS CRABBE GAVE BIRTH TO A SON one month after the death of her husband. She named the boy John Arthur, in memory of him. Mr Crabbe had been overjoyed at the news of his wife's unexpected pregnancy. A middle-aged man, disappointed for many years by his wife's failure to produce a child, he was delighted at the prospect of a son who would transform the marriage he saw as adequate and comfortable into something much more satisfactory. So it was tragic that he should die before the child was born.

John Arthur was a remarkable little boy. For one thing, it was realized within 18 months of his birth that he was severely mentally handicapped. As he grew into a strapping toddler it was obvious that his mind was defective. For such a young child he had a disconcerting, rasping, even sonorous voice, which he produced from his chest in a series of garbled speeches made up of sounds not unlike real words. In spite of his mother's sustained efforts to teach John Arthur the beginnings of a vocabulary, the boy continued to clamour in his own clanging language, as though half remembering words and phrases from some distant past. He developed a shock of unruly black hair which flopped over his brow, although it did not grow to such an extent on the crown or the back of his head. Most striking of all was his bulging forehead which protruded over his eyes, shadowing them. They retreated into his head like two dangerous eels in an underwater crevice.

But Mrs Crabbe soon discovered that her growing son, so inwardly disturbed and so incommunicative, had an unusual gift. He had the power in his hands to heal. The first manifestation of this was when he came into the house from the bushes of the garden holding the broken body of a fledgling bird. It stared from his cupped hands and beat itself against his palms. But soon it became calm, even torpid. As Mrs Crabbe watched, John Arthur caressed the wound on the bird's breast until his fingers were smeared with its blood. Then he raised the tiny creature to his lips and kissed it on the crown of its head. Its eyes flickered suddenly, like gems struck from a rock. The bird hopped from the boy's hands on to the carpet. The only traces of any wound were the blood which stained John Arthur's hands and a tiny feather which clung to his lips. So Mrs Crabbe realized that her son had an affinity with wild creatures. She could hardly help noticing his tendency to bring into the house all sorts of wounded animals, birds and insects. Each time, however severely damaged the sparrow, the spider or the shrew, it was soon whole again, and happy to stay with John Arthur in his room.

The boy continued to grow sturdy. He carried himself well, if occasionally with a stoop, cultivated from the almost continual nursing of injured creatures. The mass of hair still fell on his forehead and still his eyes seemed buried under his powerful brow. John Arthur's hands were long and thin, even fragile. They held the dusty wings of a moth or the limbs of a daddy-long-legs with a tenderness which Mrs Crabbe found touching.

As she watched her son's strong body and his ponderous head hunched over his latest find she marvelled at the gentleness of his fine fingers. Then she felt her love for John Arthur and her regret for her dead husband mingling and aching inside her.

The boy did not go to school. Instead, he stayed at home and tended his ever-growing collection of specimens. His bedroom was full of small creatures which came and went from his window. They were not imprisoned. They were free to go, once heated by the warmth of John Arthur's fingers, but sometimes the grateful creatures would return to the boy. John Arthur could not wash or dress himself. He could not feed himself without making a fearful mess. He could not communicate with other human beings although he still held forth at length, and with a seemingly increasing vocabulary, in his own discordant language. But John Arthur had the heat in his hands and the breath from his lips to salve and restore the broken limbs of his many patients.

Naturally, word of John Arthur's power spread among Mrs Crabbe's friends, the circle that had grown up as her husband had become more successful. They had consoled her on the death of Mr Crabbe and had followed the development of John Arthur. But much as Mrs Crabbe enjoyed the company of her friends, she often felt that their interest in her and her curious son was ghoulish. She imagined them discussing John Arthur with a sort of unhealthy relish whenever she was not there. She could hear them describing the inhabitants of his bedroom, the voles, the mice and the moths, the leathery bat and the ducking, sidling jackdaw which never blinked. Mrs Crabbe particularly resented the dashing Mrs Sylvester, who pried into John Arthur's every small sign of progress, who chuckled at his rasping cries. She was gaudy, metallic. Mrs Crabbe resented her almost predatory interest in the boy.

Mrs Sylvester had a son who was as pert as herself. He was a success at school, regarding his fellows with a lift of his eyebrows and a mocking smile. Sometimes he accompanied his mother on her visits to Mrs Crabbe's house, but he was plainly uncomfortable in the presence of John Arthur. He flushed under the distant gaze of John Arthur's eyes and seemed overwhelmed, dominated by the weight of John Arthur's brow. But his mother remained jaunty, and her son gained in confidence until he, too, had developed a kind of growing curiosity about the power of John Arthur's fragile hands.

Then tragedy struck the Sylvester family. Within a few hours of being bright and swift, Mrs Sylvester's son fell gravely ill. He lay inert on his bed, his eyes open but unseeing. The doctors diagnosed that the boy had had the seed of a tumour growing within his skull, unsuspected until now. With the sudden pressure of the tumour against his brain, he was immediately paralysed in every limb. Furthermore, the tumour, at present the size of a small fist, would continue to grow, unclenching like a fist threatening to burst within the boy's head. He would die. Meanwhile, he lay with his eyebrows raised and with his mouth fixed in the faint smile which he had so often carried in the swift brightness of his health. More doctors were consulted. All of them were pessimistic, even advising against the boy's removal from the house to a hospital. It would be in vain; better to leave him lying on his own bed, breathing faintly and with the hard smile caught on his lips.

One evening Mrs Crabbe was astonished, on answering the door, to see the figure of Mrs Sylvester standing in the porch. The powerful, still glinting woman held the motionless body of her son in her arms. She stepped silently into the house. John Arthur stood at his mother's elbow and watched the progress of the woman who came into the hall. His chin was up, his eyes caught the light and threw it back at the limp boy in Mrs Sylvester's arms. There was an electric, crackling interchange between the sunken eyes of John Arthur and those of the unseeing, dying boy. And instantly John Arthur began to chatter in his harsh voice, releasing a torrent of half recognizable, half remembered sounds. Mrs Crabbe followed her son towards his bedroom and Mrs Sylvester carried her son behind them.

John Arthur opened his door. As he went into the room there started from all corners of the darkness the whispers of his other patients. Mrs Sylvester swallowed her apprehension and advanced towards the bed. She placed her motionless son on it. Still John Arthur poured out his dry, shouting sounds, echoed around the room by the rustling of the bat and the crow, the movement of the mole and the moth. Then Mrs Crabbe took Mrs Sylvester firmly by the arm and led her back to the door, out of the room. They left John Arthur and the stricken boy alone, in the muttering darkness.

John Arthur's cries stopped as the door closed. The two women waited outside the room, looking away from each other, along the corridor. Then, as though no time had passed at all, they were woken from their confusion, their doubts, by a barely perceptible click as the door opened and slowly swung wide. The light from the hallway spilled into the bedroom. John Arthur stood near his bed. His hair swept back from his brow, his eyes challenged the light, boldly staring towards the door.

There was no one, no figure, no boy lying on the bed. Only the rumpled blankets showed the imprint of a body. Two things seemed to happen as one, two outbursts of sound and colour simultaneously. Up from the bed there rose the metallic brightness of a bird, a jay. It beat across the room, blue, black, white and blue again. The jay struck the mirror with a loud crack, a dazzling duplicate of itself, dropping to the carpet and releasing a torrent of guttural shrieks. At the same time, with a mocking smile on his lips, John Arthur Crabbe began to speak in a clear, measured voice, welcoming his mother.

DREAMCATCHER

I'D DRIVEN ALMOST TO PASADENA before I'd had time to think about what I was doing and where I was going. The previous few days in the office had been a stress-filled haze, and I was still muddling over them as I headed down the freeway out of LA. I just needed to get out of LA. The snow was high on the San Bernardino range and its lower flanks, towards the Mojave desert.

I'd been embroiled in 'development hell' . . . a script-writer's nightmare, where the concepts of story and feasible scenario collide headlong and grind to a standstill, like the coming together of tectonic plates. My editor and the studio executives hadn't exactly seen eye to eye . . . and after hours and days of wrangling debate they'd sent me to take a break, to spend a weekend relaxing by the pool in a faraway hotel.

Three hours from the city of eight million people, the air was fresh and clear and the landscape was uncluttered by human civilization . . . apart from the acres and miles of windmills across the undulating plain west of the highway. There was something oddly ominous about their gleaming white towers and the slow, rhythmic turning of the vanes. On an impulse, I turned east, onto a smaller, lightly gravelled road. There was no sign, but it was well maintained and took me away from the glare of the lowering sun. I didn't know where I was going, except that the coolness of a gathering dusk felt good. After a few miles I stopped to get out and breathe . . .

The desert. A silvery blue twilight. For centuries it had been home to the Paiute people, until they'd been hassled and hustled off their lands by settlers, by miners and prospectors. More recently, the last of the Paiute would've left for the brighter lights of the big city and a search for employment along the Californian coast.

Now, only their ghosts lingered, in a wilderness inhabited by jack rabbits and rattlesnakes and the lurking, limping shadows of coyote.

The mountains had been golden, as the sun sank and set. Now they were blue and fading to grey and a deeper black. Shivering, I got back into my car. I turned on the headlights and drove further into the darkness. In the mirror I saw the last orange streak of the day I was leaving behind, and then it was gone. The world was void. Mine were the only lights in it. I was lost, but it was all right . . . I would drive and drive, I had enough fuel to drive all night, and I would stop if I saw the neon of a motel . . . or I'd pull off the road and doze in the car, huddle in a warm jacket, listen to some lonesome lost-in-the-desert music and snuggle up with the bottle of rum I'd brought along for company.

Music . . . as I thought of it I took my eyes off the tunneling headlights and fumbled at the buttons on the radio. The channels whined and chattered. A pulse of rock 'n' roll which was too much of the city I was trying to escape . . . a jabber of voices . . . a second or two of a nasal southern country voice and steel guitar . . .

And then, when I glanced back at the road, there was something on it.

On the road. In the middle of the road. A dark shape.

I slammed my foot onto the brake. The dark shape lifted and shifted and changed, became two dark shapes.

One of the shapes, something dead and broken, stayed where it was. The other lifted off, with a sudden heaving struggle of dark wings.

Too late to stop in time, too late to swerve, I felt the car bump over the dead shape in the road. The other shape smashed onto the windscreen. Then it disappeared, a cartwheeling clatter of wings and beak and talons, over the roof of the car.

I stopped and got out, walked back.

The thing in the road, which had already been stinking dead for a day or two days, was even worse for wear now that I'd run over it. A deer? A mule? In the red tail-lights and the coiling fume of the exhaust, it was a horribly misshapen affair of hooves and a raggedy pelt and grinning yellow teeth.

Further back, as I walked into the darkness, there was a trail of scattered feathers. A buzzard? A scavenging, opportunistic eagle?

Whatever, it was still alive. There was a rummaging commotion in the nearby scrub. A silence. And then another shuddering struggle. Somehow, with a huge and painful effort, it lifted off and beat into the darkness. I heard the whoosh-whoosh-whoosh of its wings as it rose into the air and into the night.

Music? No thank you. Back in the car I snapped off the radio. I turned off the engine. I switched off the headlights.

I shivered and huddled into the warmth of the car seat. Utter inky blackness. No stars, no moon. No world. Sounds? None at all. I sat and settled myself, quite calm and unflustered and strangely comfortable with the unworldliness of the silent darkness which folded around me. Experimentally, I squeezed my eyes shut. No difference.

And yet, then, when I opened them again, I could see two things. Two things which hadn't been there before . . .

On the windscreen, where the bird had struck, there was an imprint of the shape it had assumed at that moment . . . the split second of its impact. It was silvery against the night outside, against the background of the invisible mountains. Ancient . . . timeless . . . as clear and as beautifully delineated as the fossilized shape of an ancient bird, preserved for millions of years in rock. And as ephemeral as the dust it was made of. The powdered dust of the desert . . . the dust of the air . . . the dust of its own feathers . . . the very dust of itself. I could have swiped it away with one swipe of the wipers. But for now, the shape of an eagle was imprinted on the windscreen of the car.

And the other thing I saw? A glimmer of light. In the distance, or maybe only a few yards away . . . a fire.

It flickered and flared and faded, as though someone or something was moving around it and in front of it. The light of flames, in the desert.

I took my coat and my bottle of rum, I got out of the car and walked carefully through a black cold world, towards the firelight. Who could have lit it? In the dark distance I heard the howl of a coyote. I could make out the faintest outline of boulders on the skyline, eroded into enormous marbles by centuries of desert winds and flurries of rain. Who would I find at the campfire? A lone hiker, or a party of rock-climbers . . .

I stumbled and tripped in the coarse brush, turned

my ankle on the burrow of a squirrel or an owl, or
maybe the workings of a scorpion or desert spider. The
firelight flared in a breath of wind. I heard a muttering
of voices, and the bright staccato of laughter.

I came close to the fire. I called out, throwing my
voice ahead of me in greeting, not to surprise or startle
or intrude . . .

There was no one.

I stood and stared around me. I threw my voice again,
making it friendly and calm and yet firm, as though
unafraid. I waited. Perhaps they'd gone into the scrub
to collect more wood. I sat by the fire, where the sand
was smooth and warm, and I waited, ready to stand and
smile and introduce myself and hope I'd be welcome to
their hospitality.

No one came. For many long minutes . . . for an
hour? . . . I sat and stared around me, in a curious state of
anxiety and wariness, wondering who was out there and
what they were doing, if they were watching me and
wondering too. When the fire settled and collapsed into
a bed of white-hot embers, I stood and wandered and
found an armful of dead wood to refuel it. A blaze . . . it
billowed a plume of sparks into the air, it was a dazzle of
flame. I had my warm jacket, I had the companionship
of rum. I snuggled closer to the fire, to my fire, the fire
which someone had lit and brightened with voices and
laughter and then abandoned to me. I drank more rum.

At last I relaxed, unafraid of the shadows which
moved and rustled in the darkness around me. A legacy
of laughter and fire . . . a mysterious gift.

I slept. Not a dream. Not a moment of wakefulness
or wondering or troubling thought. A void of sleep.

When I awoke I was cold and aching. The fire had

gone out. It was a steely grey dawn. My bones creaked as I struggled to my knees and then stood up. The ash of the fire was still warm, but the embers had cooled hours ago. In the first light, I saw for the first time where I'd been sleeping and the miles and miles of scrub desert around me . . . the distant mountains and their rubble of boulders, a grumbling grey sky which leaned and folded onto me and the little road I'd followed, and my car, an oddly incongruous piece of machinery which I'd left a hundred yards away.

I limped back to it. The quick stink of something dead reminded me of what had happened. Remembering, I peered into the scrub for the trail of feathers I'd followed, but I couldn't see them. The car seemed like a very cold and dead thing. It didn't belong in this place. But I was glad it was there, and relieved when I opened the door and a warm light came on inside it. I sat at the wheel.

I turned the key in the ignition. I turned on the headlights. For a few moments I marvelled at the imprint on the windscreen. An eagle . . . its shape was as big as the piece of glass it had struck, and the dust of its wings had hardened and set with the dew of a desert night. Ancient, as ancient as a fossil locked in stone . . . a miracle, the detail of its feathers, its breast and wings and the splayed-out plumes of its tail as it had tried to swerve and avoid the impact . . . perfectly defined, as though forever and ever.

And yet, one swipe of the wipers and it was gone. The screen was clear and empty. Nothing but a grey landscape of scrub and the chilly grey mountains.

Ready to drive, I glanced into the mirror.

Someone had been in the car. While I'd been waiting

by the fire, settling to its warmth and enjoying a dream-less sleep, someone had been in the car and . . .

Another gift. There was a web, dangling from the mirror. A cobweb, fashioned in wood and strips of leather. And, woven into it, the feathers of an eagle . . . as though caught in the web, like the memory of a dream I'd had.

Printed in the USA
CPSIA information can be obtained
at www.ICGtesting.com
CBHW010006300124
3843CB00022B/1211

9 781948 405423